Praise for *The H*

4 1/2 Roses "Rachel is the first Huntress along with her husband Matthew. The incredible Rachel is the only one to volunteer to help her husband fight the monsters. ...Matthew has come back for his love, even though he did not know how Rachel would receive him. They are a dynamic couple. The Huntress is a great addition to those who follow the Hunter series and will be an addition to my must read again titles. Thank you, Ms. Walker for continuing to amaze us with this series. " ~ *Noemi, A Romance Review*

4 Stars "...This is a very interesting new spin on Ms Walker's Hunters, one that is enjoyable and a great read for paranormal fans ...Shiloh Walker's The Huntress is sure not to disappoint! " ~ *Elizabeth, Euro Reviews*

"...THE HUNTRESS totally rocks in my book... Scoot on over to Samhain Publishing and purchase your copy of THE HUNTRESS today. You won't be disappointed." ~ *Sinclair Reid, Romance Reviews Today*

Praise for *Hunter's Pride*

4 Angels "...Hunter's Pride immediately draws the readers in with Kennedy's struggle and Duncan's compassion for a little girl. Readers remain hooked through the entire story by two characters that are realistic, genuine, and someone to cheer for. The plot is riddled with dangerous situations and portrays the drive to find the one thing you need to have the life you want, whether it is someone or something. With a twist along the way, Duncan and Kennedy's journey to be complete is one that this reader found to be pleasurable, sizzling passionate, and heartfelt. Shiloh Walker has done a tremendous job at earning herself a new fan. This reader will be searching for another book with her name on it. 4 Angels!" ~ *Jessica, Fallen Angel Reviews*

5 Stars "Hunter's Pride is a great sensual paranormal romance. Ms. Walker's dialogue is stimulating and suspenseful, yet evocative. ...If you'd like to read a quick stand alone erotic paranormal romance, which is set amid the world of The Hunters series, then I'd recommend you read Hunter's Pride" ~ *KayleeMarie Walker, Just Erotic Romance Reviews*

4 Red Hearts "...I found Hunter's Pride by Shiloh Walker to be a very enjoyable read. Hunter's Pride blends great characters with a unique storyline into an unforgettable tale that grabs your attention from the start and holds it until the very end. The sexual interactions between Kennedy and Duncan were very hot and sensation in nature. If you are looking for an intense story with lots of passion to satisfy your paranormal appetite, then look no further." ~ *Contessa, The Romance Studio*

Praise for *Malachi*

"Malachi is an interesting look into how one of Shiloh Walker's most sexy Hunters got his start. I enjoyed learning about his life before we met him in the Hunter books. Malachi is a strong and sexy warrior who seems to have a heart that cannot stand to see mistreatment of the weak. ...Shiloh Walker continues to make me salivate over her incredibly hot Hunters. I love Shiloh and her Hunters!!!" ~ *Gracie, Joyfully Reviewed.com*

"Shiloh Walker writes an emotional and intriguing story with MALACHI, whetting the reader's appetite for more." ~ *Sinclair Reid, Romance Reviews Today*

3 Cups "...Malachi is another winner for Ms Walker. I look forward to reading more of her works." ~ *Matilda, Coffee Time Romance*

Legends

Hunters and Heroes

By Shiloh Walker

A Samhain Publishing, Ltd. publication

Samhain Publishing, Ltd.
2932 Ross Clark Circle, #384
Dothan, AL 36301

Legends: Hunters and Heroes
ISBN: 1-59998-208-0
First print publication date: July 2006
www.samhainpublishing.com

First The Huntress electronic publication: January 2006
First Hunter's Pride. electronic publication: February 2006
First Malachi. electronic publication: May 2006

Legends
Hunters and Heroes

The Huntress

A tale of vampire beginnings from

Every hero has a past...

And every legend has a beginning.

Chapter One

They gathered in the dark. Oil lamps lit the darkness of Rachel's small home. The meager light wasn't anything they counted on to battle back the monsters outside—one particular breed of monster, only Rachel's own faith would keep out.

The other, nothing could keep out, but those particular monsters didn't care for fire or strength. And there were enough men within the small structure to keep them away. Those wolf-creatures fed on fear, it seemed. And although the men and women here were very frightened, they were also determined.

Something had to be done.

They just didn't know what.

The children slept in the back room, while the adults gathered in the front to speak in hushed tones. None of them liked leaving their homes, especially not at night, but they couldn't be seen gathering, not like this, not to speak of these— these things. If they were, they could be seen as devils, or monsters.

Not as the people who were fighting to rid the land of them.

They were losing though.

Matthew hadn't been seen in months. Rachel's husband, they knew, was likely dead. If Matthew—that strong, powerful man—so unafraid, so wise, had fallen to these wicked, unnatural creatures, it was only a matter of time.

Had God deserted them?

Ezekiel lifted rheumy eyes, staring at Rachel. Like so many times, she stood staring out the narrow slit of the window, as though she waited still for Matthew's return.

Poor woman, how frightened she must be. She lived in the very outskirts of town, so far away from all others, so alone. She refused to come and live closer to town. Refused all offers of help. They knew she still clung to her hopes that Matthew would return.

Closing his eyes, he prayed, *God, what are we to do now...*

It seemed there wasn't going to be an answer. There hadn't been. Not for months and months. The odd twisted creatures—half wolf, half man—had been appearing more and more often, taking more and more of the people from the town, killing man, woman and child alike. Worse, some of the people attacked didn't die.

Some survived. Only to turn into the monsters on the next full moon.

And other monsters—pale creatures that came only at night, creatures that could beguile you with a look. Creatures that sank teeth into a person's neck and fed, draining the lifeblood from them. Some died. Others arose to become just like the pale things that had bitten them.

Zeke shook his head, folding his hands atop his cane and resting his chin on them. What were they going to do...

Samuel spoke. "Things have gotten worse, even since we spoke three days ago. We are still two weeks until the full moon but already the men hunting have seen three of the wolf-beasts."

Rachel said quietly, "You sit here in terror, speaking in the dark. You have to do something."

"Woman, be silent," Samuel said wearily. "I know you grieve for your man, but this is something we must handle."

She laughed bitterly. "Like you have handled it since Matthew disappeared? Talking in the dark, sending men out to search but not kill?"

Samuel rose, shaking his head. "You are a woman. You do not even know what you are speaking of. We are hunting them, trying to learn where they hide, what their weaknesses are."

Spinning around, she glared at him, hands fisted at her side. She shoved back the cloth that covered her head as she crossed the room. Samuel stepped back, but she didn't move to him. Instead, she went to the fire and leaned down, grabbing a flaming piece of wood from the fire.

The dancing flames cast eerie shadows on her face as she turned and stared at them. "*This* is their weakness. The fire. It is all Matthew took with *him* when he left. Fire. And night after night, he returned, unharmed, victorious. He burned them. Both the wolf-things and the pale monsters burn. The pale things fear sunlight and wood—they cannot take wood in the heart. He has killed them just with pieces of wood. Sticks, you fool. *Those* are their weaknesses and he told you this time and again and yet you still will not fight as he fought. You cowards."

It had been Matthew who had discovered one of the creatures' weaknesses.

They all knew how the pale things and the wolf-creatures alike fled from fire, recoiling in terror at the sight of burning flame. One of the warriors, long dead, had been the first one to actually use flame as a weapon.

But the wood...*that* had been divine intervention. One of the pale creatures had fought Matthew, wounding him, nearly killing him. Just as the pale one had launched himself at Matthew, the warrior had grabbed a thick tree limb from the ground. The end had been jagged, and Matthew had held that nasty pointed edge toward the pale one.

The pale one's speed had propelled him onto the limb and he fell down, lifeless.

Weapons of stone and metal had no effect of the creatures. But wood—wood had killed one.

"Wood, you fools. Wood, fire, sunlight," Rachel repeated, her voice low and angry. "Fools."

Samuel's face reddened with fury as a mere woman faced him down with rage in her eyes. Advancing on her, he made as though to speak when Ezekiel rose. The oldest among them, all eyes turned to him and even Samuel's eyes dropped when Zeke spoke. "Rachel is right. We cannot keep hiding in the shadows. Matthew was our greatest warrior. But he is gone. We cannot keep waiting and watching in silence. If we are to save our town, we must act now and stop this pointless...whatever it is we have done since we have lost him."

"Ezekiel—"

Zeke just looked at Samuel and shook his head. "No, Samuel. We tried it your way for a time. Now it is done. We must find the warriors within ourselves if we are to even stand a chance at saving ourselves." Turning his head, he stared at Rachel. The woman still stood, glaring at Samuel with rage in her eyes, the flickering torch still clutched in her fist.

At first glance, she looked to be a vision of strength, of power. But she trembled. Zeke couldn't even imagine the pain that must be tearing through her. But still, she stood tall and carried on. She would, until the last breath left her body. She believed in what Matthew had started. She would fight.

If she had but been born a man...

There was a knock at the door.

All fell silent. Rachel licked her lips, her eyes dropping to the torch in her hands. "A moment, please," she called out. Her voice was steady as if she had just been discussing how unusually dry the weather had been of late. Quickly, she turned and threw the torch back into the fire as the men and women silently moved and filed into the underground chamber. In the back room, the two women that had been assigned to watch the children were doing the same with them. It took only a handful of moments. Ezekiel held the lamp as they crouched down in the darkness and they all prayed silently, as they had never prayed before.

If somebody suspected anything was amiss, they would lose yet another.

Not to the monsters, but to the town.

Too many had been killed. If not by the monsters, then by their own neighbors for heresy.

✦✦✦✦✦✦

Nerves danced in her belly as she moved to the door.

Pressing one hand against it, she tried to make it sound as though she had been wakened from a sleep. "Who is it?"

"Rachel...it is Matthew."

Time halted.

Rachel could swear that her breath, her heart, even the blood within her body stopped flowing. Nothing mattered, except that voice—that familiar, precious voice.

She started to tear at the latch, but then common sense intruded.

How...

It had been months since Matthew had been seen.

No trace of him had been found. She had even gone into the woods to search for him.

No bit of clothing, not his knife, nothing.

It was like he had never existed.

Except she dreamed of him. She remembered how it had felt to have him pressed against her in the night, the feel of his body against hers, how he had kissed her, how he had loved her.

"Matthew..." she whispered brokenly.

"Open the door, Rachel."

Tears rolled down her face. She couldn't. If he was here after all this time, then it was because he was one of them. The pale creatures.

"I-*I-*" Something was wrong. She felt in her heart.

"Rachel." His voice was husky, imploring. "Open the door, let me talk to you."

"I-I can't. Where have you been?"

She heard him sigh. "It's a long story, love. Please."

Licking her lips, she whispered, "Were—were you attacked?"

Silence. And then finally, a guttural whisper, "Yes. Yes, I was."

She fell keening to the ground, wrapping her arms around her middle as though to keep the pain inside from tearing her apart. *No,* she prayed silently, lifting her eyes heavenward. *Not my Matthew.*

"Rachel, please. You don't understand. There are things I need to tell you. I know the people are in there. We need to talk. All of us. There's not much time."

"Go away!" she sobbed.

By this time, they had heard and she could feel the men and women behind her. Ezekiel knelt down behind her stroking her hair. "Rachel, what is it?"

She lifted tear drenched eyes to his. "Matthew—they got Matthew..."

Samuel drew the sword from his back, lifting it to the door. "Whatever you do, Rachel, do not invite him in."

From outside, they all heard a sarcastic laugh and then Matthew said, "Samuel, you lack-witted fool. That is my home. I do not need an invitation to enter my own home. The only reason I wait to enter is so that I do not frighten my friends."

Rachel pressed her face against Ezekiel's shoulder and sobbed.

Ezekiel, however, studied the door with thoughtful eyes. There was nothing...compelling in that man's voice. He had fought too many of these creatures, ever since they had first appeared in the lands some fifty years ago. They had come from the east and they could compel a person with just a word and if a weak soul was fool enough to be lulled by one of them, he was done for.

After five decades, Ezekiel had learned to resist that compulsion. Prayer was the strongest resistance and strength in soul and spirit would guide you through. Wouldn't keep the thing from killing you, but it may save you from having it take your soul when it killed you.

Or so they had thought.

Matthew had the strongest soul of any man he had ever met.

But Matthew had been taken.

"What has happened to you, Matthew?" he asked guardedly.

"Ezekiel, many things. Many, many things, but I am still the man you have known since you taught me how to hunt," came the familiar voice, one full of weariness.

He lifted his head and caught the gaze of one of the frightened women. Ruth came over and knelt by Rachel. She wrapped the younger woman in her arms and murmured quietly to her.

Ezekiel rose slowly, old bones popping and creaking. He moved to the door, resting a hand on it. He prayed, uncertain of what he should do. In his heart, part of him had hoped and prayed along with Rachel that Matthew had been miraculously returned to them.

God would not be so cruel as to answer that prayer like this, sending the man back a monster.

No. No, He would not.

No. Straightening his shoulders, Ezekiel looked back at his friends. Their faces were filled with varying degrees of shock, fear and hope.

"My friends, he can enter whenever he wants. It is his home. Let us see why he has come."

Slowly, he opened the door.

The man who stood there looked much as he always had, long black hair that hung past his shoulders, his handsome face a bit paler than before, but Ezekiel saw the same man he had seen months ago, when Matthew had left one night to battle the monsters. Left and never returned.

Matthew's blue eyes held a faint glow as he stared at Rachel, crouching on the floor, refusing to look at her husband.

He looked exactly as he always had, just more pale. And although his eyes glowed like blue fire in his face, they lacked the unholy light they had seen in so many of the monsters they had all faced.

"Rachel..."

Rachel stiffened. Lifting her eyes, she looked at him, tears rolling down her face. He moved toward her, but when she started to crawl away, he stilled. His eyes closed and Ezekiel watched as powerful strong hands closed into useless fists.

Oh, he had become one of them, Ezekiel could feel it. Those *things* felt different.

But there was also something unique about him. He still felt like the same man.

The men and women Ezekiel had known who had been changed no longer felt the same. He knew people. He'd always had a—sense for them, for lack of a better word. It was like what had made them human had simply drained out of them along with their blood as they became the monsters.

But Matthew, it was like he was still Matthew. Full of grief as he stared at his young wife, and just as in love with her as the day they had married.

Gently, Ezekiel cleared his throat.

Matthew turned to face him, forcing a small smile. "Hello, old man."

"Matthew." To his shock, he felt tears choking him. "It is...good to see you, boy."

Behind them, Samuel hissed. "He's one of *them!*"

Matthew turned and glared at Samuel. "You'd best be silent. You have cost the lives of countless people with your fool ways over the past months, Samuel and you'll be lucky if I do not beat you bloody for it."

Samuel took one step toward Matthew. In his hand, he held a wooden crucifix. All of the monsters feared that simple wooden symbol. Matthew, though, just smiled. "I have nothing to fear from the symbol of our Lord, Samuel. I am not one of the damned. I didn't seek or welcome this change, nor have I turned into a murdering maniac. And you and I will have a reckoning for the lives you have cost. But I'm not here to deal with you tonight."

Enraged, Samuel lifted one of the oil lamps from the table and lobbed it at Matthew. Matthew batted it aside and took one step toward Samuel. All in the room gasped as Matthew's eyes began to swirl and glow. "Sit down, Samuel. Be silent and sit before I lose my temper."

The other man fell to the rush-strewn floor, his eyes glazed.

Matthew turned back to Ezekiel, his mouth grim. "Dark times have come, Zeke. Very dark." His eyes closed and a shudder passed through him. "Their numbers multiply, more and more with every moonrise."

Ekekiel said quietly, "I know."

Matthew shook his head. "No. You cannot possibly understand just how many will rise in the coming days. For a time, they were isolated—we kept them trapped right here.

But they have moved beyond our borders, into the lands beyond the sea, spreading farther and farther, despite how we fought to stop them. It is time that we face them on their own ground."

A quiet, dark man named Judas stepped from the back. Few liked him, simply for the name he was given at birth. He was as loyal and true as the sun, but because of the name... Matthew looked at him with a lifted brow. "Jude?"

"What is this you speak of, Matthew? Facing them how?"

Matthew took a deep breath and it seemed to Ezekiel that he didn't wish to speak at all. A great burden seemed to rest on those strong shoulders. What was it that troubled him so?

Dear God, give me courage.

Matthew didn't want to be here. Closing his eyes, he reached inside for strength. It didn't come from within, though.

He felt a warmth. Like summer sunshine. He hadn't seen the sunshine in months, and wouldn't see it again—unless he was ready to die by it. But when he opened his eyes, there, just out of his field of vision, was a warm golden glow. If he tried to turn his head and catch it, he would see nothing.

Time seemed to have stopped. The faces of the people before him had stilled and none of them seemed to be breathing, blinking—they weren't aware of him at all.

"What is this you have done?"

The voice seemed to come from all around, echoing everywhere, making his heart tremble. *I have done nothing. You just needed a moment to prepare. You were given one.*

Matthew shook his head. "I don't know that I can do this thing you ask me. How can I tell them that in order to destroy these monsters we must become like them?"

You are not like them, Matthew. You are the same man you were the night you walked in the woods to fight them. And it was the strength, the courage, the faith that is in your heart that brought you through—the same will see them through.

"Benjamin..." His voice trailed off as he lifted his hands and stared at them. They looked the same. Exactly the same. But just last night, he had used these hands to rip apart one of the wolf-creatures. Rip it apart, limb by limb. The wolf-creatures had taken a child from his home. Would have eaten the poor boy. Matthew had taken the child back, knocked on the door and watched until the father dared to open the door. At first, the father had been afraid, afraid of his own child. Afraid the child was a monster.

Matthew would have rather taken the child inside and placed him sleeping in the bed, but his new body...he was a pale one now. He could enter no home without an invitation save his own. "Benjamin, how can we do this?"

The angel's voice echoed from everywhere. *Because if you do not, the foulness will spread unchecked across the land. Warriors will come, Matthew. People who will stand and battle against these monstrosities. Make no mistake about that.*

But would you wait when you know you can make a difference now?

Will you let these people suffer? You can start turning the tide—here, now. Will you let these people perish when you and these men and women inside can save them? Or will you wait until another band of warriors stands ready? It may be a year

*before more men and women are found ready to fight. A decade.
Centuries.*

Matthew turned away, weary. Pressing his brow against the
door, he muttered, "You know I cannot do that."

The bright golden glow increased and a wind drifted
through the room, almost like the breeze that drifted through a
summer meadow. *Yes, I know.* The glow faded, and with it, the
warmth of the angel's presence.

But Matthew, once more, was resolute.

As he turned to face his friends, he straightened his
shoulders.

There was a reason he had survived the attack so many
months ago. And if this was it, by God, he would see it through.

Chapter Two

"How many?" Nicholas demanded, his eyes wide with fear. He was hardly more than a boy. Both his parents had been killed, his father by the wolf-creatures. His mother had been struggling to provide for herself and her sons, but then one night, the pale monsters came. When the call came, she couldn't resist and she walked out the door.

But it hadn't been to her death.

It had been Nicholas who had been forced to kill her three days later when she came back. She had tried to rape him, her own son. He had a nasty, ugly bite mark on his neck, but the worst scars were inside.

Rachel wanted to offer him comfort, but she was too afraid. For most of the night, Matthew had talked. The monsters had spread far beyond their borders, flooding what remained of the Roman Empire, traveling eastward over the seas, traveling south, north...like locusts.

Fear had her entire body shaking. Staring at Matthew, she waited to hear him answer. She was a simple woman—numbers meant little to her. Matthew had been educated. Ezekiel had seen to that. Once, long ago, Ezekiel had been an important man. What had happened, she didn't know. But the old man had taught many things to Matthew.

Nicholas wasn't asking for numbers, she knew. He wanted to know if they could fight the many monsters hid within the woods, if they had the strength of arms.

As Matthew lifted glittering eyes, she saw the answer there before any of the others could understand.

No. They couldn't.

"There are many, Nicholas. Even if every man in this village was willing to fight, there would not possibly be enough."

And those were just the ones that hadn't moved on.

Voices rose and the men began to speak urgently amongst themselves. Women began to whisper. Some began to weep in silence. And a few even began to cry openly.

Rachel rose. Her hair flowed down her back. Her feet moved along the rushes as she wove through the people, making her way toward Matthew.

He heard her coming. She knew he did, even though he had his back to her. She could see it in the way he tensed, the way his hand closed into one tight fist. "Why didn't you come back?" she whispered.

Patiently, she waited for him to turn and face her. Rachel wanted to look into his eyes, needed to. But he didn't turn around. "I could not."

"Why?" she asked baldly.

"I could not. I had to learn..." his voice trailed off and slowly, he turned.

All voices fell silent as he turned to look at her. Rachel flushed as she felt people watching them, but she didn't care. She had to know why he hadn't come back to her. His hand lifted, reaching up. She gasped as his flesh touched hers, the coolness of his flesh—the coolness of death. One roughened fingertip touched her neck and she swallowed as he felt the fluttering pulse there. "I could not," he repeated, his eyes locked on the wildly beating pulse. "Not until I knew I could trust myself. You see, I am still a man. But now, I battle the hungers of a monster, Rachel. I had to wait until I knew you would be safe from those hungers."

He wanted to touch her—touch her like he hadn't been able to touch her in months. The silken feel of her skin under his fingers wasn't enough. She smelled soft and sweet. The long, black sweep of her hair hung around her shoulders like a cloak—his hands itched to touch it, while at the same time, he wanted to hide her away so that none of the men there could see her. His Rachel. His woman. His wife—he hadn't made love to her in months. Hadn't spread her thighs and pushed inside her body...

Hot, blistering need tore through him and his fangs started to ache inside their sockets. Blood started to pound heavily. His cock throbbed and the longer he stared at Rachel, the more he hurt. The pulse in her neck fluttered and her heartbeat sped up as their gazes locked.

They could have stood alone in the crowded room as she stared up at him. "Matthew?" she whispered.

Clenching his jaw, Matthew tortured himself a little more as he breathed in more of her warm scent. "I did come back, Rachel," he murmured, cupping her cheek in his hand. He rubbed his thumb across her lip, watching as her lashes fluttered closed.

Then he forced himself to turn away before his control snapped.

Ezekiel was watching him with those measuring eyes and Matthew jerked his gaze away. "Indeed you did come back," the old man mused, folding gnarled hands around his cane. "Why don't you tell us all, Matthew? You are holding back."

Fear had dried the spit in her mouth.

"A way to become like them."

A way to become like them...

The words echoed over and over in her head.

He was mad. He had gone mad. Rachel stood staring at Matthew, her arms wrapped around her middle as she listened to him speak.

"You cannot be serious," Nicholas whispered, tears making his young eyes bright.

"Matthew, they are cursed." Jude turned away, refusing to look at Matthew. Others wouldn't even speak to him.

Ezekiel murmured, "It must be possible to become as strong as they are without becoming the monster. You stand before me as proof, Matthew."

Rachel watched as Matthew nodded curtly.

Ezekiel closed his eyes and sighed. When the old man opened them, he lifted his eyes heavenward and whispered, "I prayed for an answer—I prayed for help. I did not expect it to come in this form."

Matthew laughed bitterly and Rachel felt tears sting her eyes. They had all prayed for help. None of them had realized the cost, though.

"I'll do it."

"You cannot, Zeke."

Ezekiel's eyes narrowed and he rose slowly, glaring angrily at Matthew as he demanded, "And I'd like to know why not, boy."

"You are old, Ezekiel. Your time in this world is nearing its end... I can feel it somehow."

Even though nothing changed on Matthew's face as he spoke, Rachel felt the pain in his words as he spoke to Zeke. The old man was the closest thing that Matthew had to a father.

Tears burned her eyes and she moved forward, wrapping an arm around Zeke.

Ezekiel just continued to glare stubbornly at Matthew. "Even if you can feel it, what does that have to do with anything?"

Matthew smiled. "If your body was still as strong as it was ten years ago, it wouldn't matter at all. And if your body was as strong as your soul, it wouldn't matter. But your body is getting weak. The body has to be strong or it won't survive the Change."

Ezekiel's shoulders slumped and for once, he looked weary. Rachel hugged him and he smiled at her. "All is well, Rachel. Our prayers have been answered, after all. We have a way to fight them, finally. Something besides huddling in the dark."

With that, he turned to face the men and women who were, arms wrapped around each other in the dark corners of the room. "Who is willing?" he asked of the men. "We have strong men here. We have all lost people to these monsters. Wives, children, mothers, fathers."

Husbands, Rachel thought starkly as nobody answered.

As the silence continued, Ezekiel started to walk through the room. "We have a chance here. We must have strength to fight them. Our prayers have been answered. God sent back our warrior—Matthew is stronger now than he ever was, and just as true. And yet you all stand there as cowards."

"Zeke," Matthew said quietly, shaking his head. "They are right to be frightened."

Rachel said flatly, "We've all been frightened. Ever since *they* came here. We've lived in fear. The men and women your age...you were born in fear. The children we have now live in fear. How can we expect that to stop unless we are willing to do something?"

Samuel whispered harshly, "We *are* doing something. But becoming monsters ourselves?"

Rachel spun to face him, her hands fisted at her sides. "My husband is *not* a monster. He is the same man he was when I married him. On the inside—I see that man when I look in his eyes. The monsters are the things out there that make me afraid to walk outside in my garden at night. That make you afraid to fish before the sun rises. Those are the monsters and Matthew offers us a way to take back our lives and none of you will dare say yes."

Her heart pounded in her chest. Her head felt strange. God, do *I* dare? she wondered. The tears that had threatened to fall most of the night finally broke free.

The life she had once known was over. It had ended the night Matthew hadn't returned all those weeks ago.

Quietly, she asked, "What would they have to do?"

For the longest time, he wouldn't tell them. And when he did, the men and women looked even more terror-stricken. The pounding in her head increased and her heart raced so hard, she could hardly breathe. She wiped her damp palms on the long cloth of her robes as she paced, listening to him speak.

It sounded horrifying.

Disgusting.

Dangerous.

Frightening.

Could a person possibly survive it, she wondered.

Moving off to the side, Rachel watched surreptitiously from the shadows as he spoke—she hoped that Matthew had no idea just how closely she was listening. He wouldn't allow her to do it.

Women had survived what the monsters had done. She'd seen them.

As Matthew had finished talking, Ezekiel turned and faced the men once more. "Who among you has the courage?" he asked quietly.

One man did bow his head and start to stand, but his wife clung to his arm. Rachel moved forward. "Jude, no. Ruth has need of you. She's lost too much already."

Matthew turned, his eyes narrowing as he looked at Rachel, but she wondered if maybe he saw something in her eyes. He studied her thoughtfully and then looked back at Jude and murmured agreement. "Indeed, Jude. A man should be able to spend both day and night with his wife."

When no other man made move to rise, Ezekiel said, "So we have not one soul brave enough?"

Rachel swallowed. "I am."

And before Matthew could say a word, she took a knife. Lifting her eyes, she forced a smile at him. "You'd never agree, love."

Strength, speed, agility—all these things he had, and he couldn't move fast enough to stop his wife from slashing her smooth flesh with a knife. The ripe, rich, sweet scent of her blood called to the monster inside of him even as anguish ripped his heart wide open.

He caught her as she stumbled. Blood fountained out. He clamped his hand over her wrist, squeezing until he had staunched the blood flow. "You little fool!" he bellowed.

She stared up at him, her eyes stark in her pale face. "Do it, Matthew. The life I once knew is over. I cannot live like this, not without you."

"Rachel," he whispered. "No." Lifting his head, he found all of them just staring at her. "Zeke, get me something to bandage her wrist with."

Zeke arched a brow. "You asked for one willing, Matthew, my friend. You were given an answer. I am sorry you weren't prepared for it."

Matthew snarled, infuriated. Enraged, he reached out, catching the front of Zeke's shirt and dragging the old man forward. "She is not a warrior."

Zeke arched a brow. "Why? Because she is a woman? Or because she is your wife?"

"Not my wife!"

Calm eyes held his. "So another man's would be acceptable? Nicholas has two young brothers, hardly more than babies that he has to take care of. Is he acceptable? Why? Because he is a man? What about Jude? He is all his wife has. She has a new baby. The monsters killed her family. She has nobody in town—without Jude, where will she go? But is Jude acceptable? Who are you to decide?"

Matthew growled. *No.* He wouldn't do this. Not Rachel.

But the ultimate decision, it would seem, wasn't going to be his.

That odd eerie silence fell again. The warm spring breeze, smelling of sunshine and flowers filled the room. "I'm cold, Matthew," Rachel whispered. "Do it, please... I smell flowers..."

Matthew closed his eyes. "Benjamin. Not her."

The angel laughed. *It wasn't my choice, Matthew. It was hers.*

Rachel smiled, lifting her face and staring past Matthew. "I would have told him that, if I thought he would have listened."

Stubborn men like him rarely listen.

Rachel said in a wry voice, "He certainly never has listened to me."

"You hear him," Matthew murmured, shaking his head. He looked back down at her wrist. Blood oozed between his fingers—the pulse pounding against his fingers felt strong and steady still, but he had to get her wrist bandaged. He couldn't keep holding the wound like this. And they had to clean it—it was deep. If they didn't keep it clean, she could lose her hand. "What were you thinking?" he said hoarsely, shaking his head.

Just that she wanted to be with you. Just that you needed somebody brave. Somebody young and strong. She made her choice. Do what needs to be done, Matthew.

Lifting his eyes, he stared at her face. Her skin hadn't even started to pale. "Let go, Matthew," she murmured. "You're holding me too tight."

He swallowed. "If I let go, you'll bleed to death."

"I have to bleed, so you can do this," she whispered.

Matthew was going to choke on the knot in his throat. Tears burned down his face as he forced his fingers to release her wrist. "Monsters shouldn't be able to cry," he muttered.

Blood start to flow once more and he watched as she opened her eyes and smiled up at him. "You're not a monster..."

No. He is not.

But nothing they said could change that Matthew felt like one as he sank his fangs into Rachel's soft flesh. And the rich, hot wine of her blood filled his belly like something so desired, so forbidden. He'd only fed on animals and the other monsters he'd hunted, never a human.

His own wife—she lay dying in his arms as he took more and more of her life blood. Her body shuddered and Matthew closed his eyes, drawing back. "She's close, isn't she?"

You do not even need me here, do you? Benjamin murmured.

Bitterly, Matthew said, "All I have ever needed is dying right in front of me."

He watched as Rachel's head hung slackly over his other arm. Their silent, still audience was still frozen and Matthew found it bitterly ironic that they were all so unaware of everything that was happening. He raised his arm, sinking his teeth into his wrist.

The blood that flowed down was deep red, far darker than it had been when he had been human. It filled her mouth, running down her cheeks, but she didn't swallow. He shifted a little, using his body to brace hers, then he placed the fingers of his uninjured hand against her neck, rubbing slowly.

"What in the hell have I done?" he muttered hoarsely as she started to swallow.

Chapter Three

It burned like fire.

The very blood within her veins was boiling, she knew it. Opening her eyes, she stared up at Matthew. Rachel was aware of each tear that fell down her face—they hurt. Breathing hurt. Her heart beating in her chest hurt.

Sweet Lord, it felt as though even the air brushing against her body hurt.

Forcing a smile, she waited until the last of the spasms faded before she dared to speak. "It is not as bad as it was."

Matthew turned his face away. "It will only get worse until you feed and you cannot feed until your fangs come," he said bleakly.

Rachel closed her eyes and resisted the urge to scream. She could have done without hearing that. But she didn't dare give in and scream, or worse—cry. Matthew looked like he was just barely clinging to sanity—his eyes were glowing. It frightened her. At the same time, though, she wanted to wrap her arms around him and hold him close. He looked lost. Her strong, brave Matthew looked so lost.

Oh, he was angry at her. She could tell. He wanted to yell at her, wanted to shake her. The fury inside him was awful, she could feel it, but he kept it under control.

Cuddling against him, she breathed in the familiar scent of his skin. They'd left their home. She barely remembered it.

Where they were now, she wasn't sure. It was a cave—dark, warm, high above the valley where their small town was nestled.

She shouldn't have felt so safe. Not out in the darkness, lacking the protection her own home provided. The wolf-creatures could come inside her home, but fire kept them at bay.

But what would keep the monsters from coming inside this cave?

Yet she felt safe—incredibly safe, alone inside these rock walls with Matthew. His hand cupped the back of her head, threading through her hair, combing out the tangles. He'd felt cool earlier, but now his body had gotten warmer and that familiar scent flooded her head, surrounding her.

The need for him that struck her in the belly caught her by surprise. Heat ripped through her—she hadn't forgotten this heat. But she hadn't ever expected to be able to satisfy it again. Not with Matthew gone.

Only he wasn't gone. He was here.

Pressing her face to his thigh, she kissed him. Her breath left her in a shaky sigh as she murmured, "Matthew, I missed you so much. I ached for you in the night and I cried, knowing you wouldn't be there. Didn't think you'd ever be there again."

His hand stilled, pressing against the back of her neck. "You need to rest," he whispered gruffly.

"No." Shaking her head, she traced her tongue against his side, pushing up his tunic. Through the coarse, rough fabric of his braies, she cupped him.

"I need my husband. I need to feel alive again. I've been dead inside since you disappeared. Bring me back to life."

At the softly murmured words, Matthew groaned. The hunger he'd kept banked inside him exploded out of control. *Selfish bastard.* His wife lay in agony, and grief and guilt choked him, but the moment she looked at him like that, he lost it.

Shaking his head, he fisted his hand in her hair and tried again to shove the monster of his own lust aside. Her mouth was moving higher up his thigh though, the hot caress of her breath driving him ever closer to madness. "Rachel, your body needs to rest while it can. You cannot understand what is happening to it. Rest..."

Fire started to dance inside his veins as she loosened the ties that held his braies up. Sliding her hand inside, she closed her hand around him and started to pump slowly up and down his length. Matthew's air left him in a hiss and he arched into her touch, staring down at her in the dim light.

"I do not want rest," she said quietly, lifting her head and staring at him. Although he knew she couldn't see him well, he could see her quite clearly. There was a glitter in her eyes that was nearly feral, very desperate. "I've done little but sleep and cry—barely existing without you. I've rested enough. I want to *live* right now."

She bent low over his lap then. Her flesh was hot, feverish from the Change raging through her and the heat of her mouth all but scalded him as she took the head of his cock inside her mouth. Without releasing him, Rachel shifted around until she had her bottom in the air and Matthew slid his hand down, palming the rounded flesh with one hand.

Hoarsely, he muttered, "You think I don't understand. Damn me to hell, but I've been lost without you. I knew all this had come to pass for a reason, and none of it mattered without you. I just wanted my life back, my wife."

She hummed softly in her throat and the vibration of it made his balls draw tight against him. "I wanted to have you with me again. If I had known these things would come, I would have taken you away from here months ago and all else be damned," he growled, his head falling back.

Hunger roused inside him and he groaned as he felt his fangs slide down, pressing against his lip. *That* hunger should have been satisfied—but the scent of Rachel's hungry body, the feel of her soft, sweet flesh under his hand, the warm wet caress of her mouth on his cock—all of it drove him to distraction. Did one hunger feed to the other, wake the other?

With his hand fisted in her hair, he tore her away from him and tumbled her to her back. "Enough," he rasped as she glared up at him petulantly. "Too long—you want to feel alive? So do I. And this is how I feel alive."

Matthew pushed her thighs apart as he shoved the long cloth of her robe to her waist. Her hair tangled around her shoulders, her face flushed with the fever, and still half-clothed, Matthew was certain she had never looked more beautiful to him. "I always knew I would come back to see you again," he whispered, lowering his mouth to kiss her gently.

She didn't want gentle, sweet kisses though. Rachel wrapped her arms eagerly around his neck and pushed her tongue greedily inside his mouth. The sharp edge of his fangs nicked her tongue but she didn't seem to care. As the taste of blood filled both of their mouths, he pushed inside her, his entire body shaking. She welcomed him—the soft, sweet recesses of her body stretching around him.

Tearing his mouth away, he pressed his brow to hers. "I knew I'd see you again," he repeated. "But I didn't dare believe that I could touch you again. I didn't pray that you'd still look at me with love in your eyes."

Her eyes narrowed and she glared at him, then slowly, the glare faded and she pushed onto her elbows, pressing her mouth to his chest.

"Ouch!"

He all but had to pry her off and she only let go of him when she chose to. Rachel stroked her hands down his chest, her lashes fluttering a little. Matthew shoved up onto his hands, staring down at the neat little circle her teeth had left on his chest before looking at her.

"I do not like it when you act like a fool, Matthew," she murmured, her lids low, her voice drowsy as she rocked her hips back and forth. "You did not think I'd look at you with love..." her voice trailed off for a moment as she looked away. Then she looked back at him and her eyes were just a little clearer. "There is nothing but love inside me for you. How can anything change that?"

Then she reached up, pressing insistently against his chest, until he rolled over, taking her with him. Rachel smiled down at him, holding his gaze with hers, as she started to rock her hips against his. "Nothing changes what is within me for you, Matthew. I have loved you since I met you. I will love you until I die..."

Her head fell back, exposing the long pale line of her throat. The savage beast of hunger tore through him and he reached up, fisted his hand in her hair and pulling her down to him. He raked her neck with his teeth, watching as a fine line of blood welled up. He licked the precious drops slowly away.

She shuddered around him, little pulsating caresses that drove him mad. Grasping her hips in his hands, he started to thrust against her harder, listening to the soft, hungry moans falling from her lips, hearing the rapid pace of her heart speeding up even more as she started to buck and plunge wildly against him.

*Alive...*her words echoed in his head and he brought her mouth to his, taking it hungrily as they both started to come.

She screamed into his mouth, her sheath clutching around his cock, squeezing and caressing his length until she had wrung him dry. Her hands clung to him, soft little whimpers occasionally escaping her even as her body slowly relaxed.

"I love you," she whispered softly.

He smiled sadly, staring up into the darkness overhead. "I love you," he murmured against her hair. She fell asleep against his chest, and he clung to her as the sun slowly rose outside.

The worse was yet to come for her—if only he could have prepared her for it.

But he could hardly stand to think of it himself.

It was worse yet as the sun rose in the sky. Retreating with her in the very depths of the cave, Matthew watched as Rachel's body arched up off the stone floor of the cave. Her fangs had yet to break through but the fever continued to rage.

Exhaustion weighed heavy on him. He wanted to sleep. The need to take his own rest was to powerful, it took all his willpower not to lie down next to her and sleep. But he couldn't.

Something was wrong.

It had been too long. Her fangs should have broken through. She needed to feed. Closing his eyes, he murmured, "Benjamin, where are you?"

There was no answer.

The angel that had given answers and comfort to Matthew in the long, dark months seemed to have deserted him. Rising, Matthew began to prowl the confines of the cave. "I shouldn't have fed her," he rasped, closing his eyes.

Behind the shield of his lids, though, he kept seeing what she had done. The blade against her wrist, the hot splash of blood, his own hungers tearing through him even as his wife's blood spilled to the ground. Pressing his hands against his face, he tried to shove the memory away.

"Damn it!" he roared.

He spun around and drove his fist into the wall, hardly even feeling the pain, even though he heard the stone walls crack, and heard bone break. Blood welled and he could feel it trickling down his clenched fist, heard drops plopping onto the ground as he stared dumbly at the wall.

Behind him, Rachel whimpered, tossing her head. Slowly, he turned, staring at her flushed face. Her eyes were opened, but she saw nothing, staring blindly up at the ceiling.

She was dying. In his gut, he knew it.

"So I am to lose you after all," he whispered brokenly, moving to her side. He sank to his knees and reached out, drawing her against him.

"Matthew..." she moaned, cuddling against him. "I am so hungry—my belly, it's empty."

He lifted his hand, staring at the blood trickling down his wrist. She couldn't feed well, not on her own at all, until her fangs broke through. But he couldn't keep her here, starving, wasting away until they came through. He placed his bloodied wrist to her mouth. "Here, sweet. This will help for a while."

Rachel turned away. "No—I want food. Matthew, food, please."

*Food...*bitter anger raged through him. "You cannot, Rachel. Not any more." Even the thought of food turned his belly.

"But I want it," she moaned. Curling up, she started to shake. "I want food—eat...eat...I want food, so hungry!" Her voice ended with a wail and when she lifted her head to stare at him, her eyes were glowing, swirling with that odd glow of power.

Did not listen to me...damned man, they never listen...men never do... Rachel rose from the floor, pacing in circles as she waited for the sun to set. There was a voice murmuring to her, a lovely, bell soft voice had circled around and around in her head.

Do not be so angry—do not curse him so, he worries for you...

"I would be fine, if he would just listen," she had muttered, ignoring the odd looks her husband had given her.

Men rarely listen, Rachel—it is just in their nature.

Oh, that man couldn't have been more right. No, Matthew didn't listen.

She needed to eat. There was an insistent little voice in her head, telling her to do just that. She couldn't explain why she had to do it, but she had to eat. Her gums itched and her jaws ached, but her belly, it was like an empty, aching pit and she needed to fill it.

He was watching her. She could feel his eyes on her, knew he was worried. But she just had to eat. Had to get some food inside her.

Had to...

The sun set.

Rachel turned, staring at Matthew. His eyes glittered and the empty knot of her belly quivered, the ache fading for a moment as a hunger of a different kind made itself known.

But then that voice started to whisper again. *Go...eat...food...*

Spinning on her heel, Rachel darted out into the night.

He caught up with her just as she hit the tree line.

Her hand closed over the apple. It wasn't ripe yet—not even close, but she didn't care. She bit into it and the sour taste flooded her mouth like the sweetest nectar. She had to fight to swallow, though. Her throat didn't want to work. Matthew's hands closed over her shoulders, his fingers biting into her skin as he shook her slightly. "Damn it, Rachel, what are you doing?"

She jerked, trying to tear away from him. Matthew wouldn't let go so she just ignored him, taking another bite of the apple. It hurt to swallow, but the knot in her belly loosened a little. The ache in her gums faded some—her mind cleared a little with each bite she took.

"Rachel, you can't feed like you're human..." Matthew murmured, but as she continued to eat the apple, his voice trailed away and his hands loosened.

Rachel dropped the core of the apple to the ground and lifted her eyes, staring up at the tree. She didn't wanted fruit.

She wanted something else. Meat. Or bread—something warm and yeasty, fresh from the oven.

Had to be something more solid. Yes, that was what she needed. Fruit was all well and good, but it wouldn't stay long in her belly. Bread and meat, that was what she needed.

"That's what I will go and find," she whispered, delicately licking away the juice from her fingers before she moved away from Matthew.

Dragging air into her lungs, she started to wander toward town. Rachel was barely aware of the ground under her feet, not even hearing Matthew moving behind her.

Everything felt so surreal. The colors of the night hadn't ever seemed this bright, this rich. The hard-packed dirt road under her feet felt dry and coarse, but her feet felt so much more sensitive and walking was almost painful. The air on her skin was a touch almost too harsh.

Everything was just too much.

The only thing that kept her from running back to the cool solitude of Matthew's cave was the hunger in her belly.

In the air was the rich smell of meat roasting. It filled her nostrils and she licked her lips, following it. It led down the path through the town, down a familiar road and when she stopped, it was a place she had seen before.

Many times. Crossing her arms, over her chest, she stood there, staring at the door, her brow wrinkled.

"Rachel, come with me *now*," Matthew demanded, his voice low and insistent.

"I'm hungry, Matthew," she murmured.

"You will not feed here."

She cast him a petulant look. "The food smells good."

It was Zeke's home.

His wife had become a monster. Matthew reached out just as the door opened, intent on grabbing her and carrying her away. What he would do with her, he didn't know—could he kill her? His own wife?

But before he could touch her, Rachel lunged forward, knocking Zeke aside.

And she entered the small home freely. The threshold posed no obstacle for her.

There was a wild, animalistic look on her face. Matthew lunged for her, but he slammed against an unseen wall at the door. "For the love of God, Zeke, invite me in," he rasped, staring at Rachel with horror.

"Come in, Matthew," Zeke said weakly as he shoved his weary body up from the ground, staring at Rachel.

Matthew entered, feeling the vestiges of whatever power kept him out of the home fall apart. He went to grab Rachel and then he stopped dead in his tracks. He hadn't even noticed the rich scent that filled the air.

But apparently it was what had Rachel so enraptured.

She was sitting in front of the fire and in her hands, she held a hunk of meat, the juice coating her hands as she sank her teeth into it. Moans of ecstasy slid from her throat with each bite. And Matthew found himself getting hard as he stood there and watched her eat.

And he was also confused as hell.

She was *eating*.

He had thought she was going to rip out Zeke's throat. She had the look in her eyes of a creature starved, staring at the door like a woman possessed.

And she had indeed come looking to feed—on human food. She'd eaten an apple. And right now, she was feasting on what was likely Zeke's dinner.

But damn it, the Change had started on her. It made no sense. The things that made her alive had changed, her heart, her breathing, even the color of her skin had changed. She was paler. Her heart was slower. The scent of her skin had changed.

She wasn't human any more.

Sinking to his knees beside her, he stared at her, watching her eat.

One thing was certain, though. Rachel wasn't wholly one of the pale creatures either.

"Matthew."

Lifting his eyes, he found Zeke staring at Rachel with a very puzzled expression on his face. "Hello, Zeke," he said tiredly, scrubbing a hand over his face.

"Matthew, I'm a little confused."

"Brother, as am I. As am I."

Zeke lowered himself onto a bench, resting his back against the wall. "She took your blood, Matthew. I remember that much before you disappeared. You have been gone for three days. By this time, she should either be a pale one, or dead."

Matthew simply arched a brow. "I know full well what should have happened by now." He looked down at Rachel. She looked completely unaware of them as she tossed down the bones, licking the juices from her fingers. Her eyes were downcast, the thick fringe of her lashes hiding her eyes from them.

Finally, she polished away the hunk of roasted meat and sighed, a look of satisfaction on her face.

She arched her back, stretching her arms over her head. Then she smiled and looked up at them, blinking sleepily.

Matthew heard Zeke's startled breath behind him. "She has Changed, Zeke," he murmured, watching as his wife from the ground. "I am just not sure what she has Changed in to."

Rachel smiled at him and then she stretched out on the floor, curling up in front of the fire like a cat.

Within moments, she was asleep.

"She is not one of you."

Matthew turned and studied Zeke. "I know I am no longer a man. I am no longer able to walk in the sun and I can no longer sit down and break bread with you. But I am not the same as one of them, either."

Zeke offered a small smile. "I am sorry, my friend. I know that—this is—this is just very strange."

Matthew sighed as he knelt down by his wife. Reaching out, he stroked a hand down the long, gleaming black banner of her hair. The fear and worry that had eaten at his gut had eased a bit, but now he was full of confusion. Driving a hand through his hair, he muttered, "Strange—that does not even begin to describe it. What is going on?"

Matthew, one day, would learn not ask such vague questions. He'd learned that Benjamin liked to arrive at just such times—if Matthew hadn't thought angels to be above such trivial behavior, he would think it amused the man.

If you wanted to know what was going on, perhaps you could have asked?

The look on Zeke's face was quite amusing—Matthew was certain he would have laughed, if he could have gotten past the surprise of realizing the old man had heard the angel speak.

"Lord be praised..." Zeke fell to the floor, pressing his face to the ground.

I am nothing so high as the Lord, Ezekiel. Just a messenger, a friend to help in these dark and troublesome times. Do not kneel before me.

"What is becoming of Rachel?"

Matthew kept his voice level and he hoped the anger he felt didn't show in his voice, but he was angry. So angry, so afraid. Nothing had gone as planned—Rachel wasn't supposed to have become a warrior. She should have been safe, lived out her life... And the Change had gone all wrong—

Actually the Change went exactly according to plan. It just was not YOUR plan.

Matthew lifted his head.

For once, just once, he would like to see this man as he spoke to him. "Benjamin, must you always speak in riddles?" he asked wearily.

The laugh that filled the room, for once, sounded a little more solid. Startled, Matthew turned and the sight that stood before him was completely unexpected.

The man that stood before him wasn't a man at all. Or just barely. Benjamin seemed hardly more than a child. The top of his head was covered with a gleaming cap of gilded curls that barely reached his shoulders.

He met Matthew's eyes and smiled. "Hello, Matthew."

Matthew couldn't speak. He just stood there and stared, his heart pounding, his throat dry and tight. Benjamin chuckled as he walked by and moved to look at Rachel. His eyes softened, sympathy moving through them. "She is having a hard time," he murmured.

Narrowing his eyes, Matthew realized he wasn't frozen after all. "Damned right, she is!"

"Matthew!" Zeke hissed, his voice full of horror and fear.

Benjamin glanced at Zeke. "He wouldn't be much of a husband if he wasn't worried for his woman, now would he?" Kneeling down by Rachel, he touched his palm to her brow. Matthew realized, that even though Benjamin looked solid enough, the boy glowed. His skin had a soft gleaming sheen to it and the light from it cast faint shadows on Rachel's skin as he touched her. She moaned at the angel's touch but then she fell silent and the lines of pain that had marred her face for days were gone. "She will rest now," Benjamin whispered, his face somber.

Rising, he turned and faced Matthew. "We need a warrior—you understand that."

"Rachel isn't a warrior."

"Why? Because she is female? Because her heart is soft and her muscles aren't as developed as yours?" Benjamin made a face. "Her heart *is* soft. And that is why we need her. Some of the people we must fight for are the ones warriors would kill out of habit. She will see them—through her eyes, you will learn to see them as well. She has strength now. She will learn to fight as well as you do, and better, because she hasn't the weaknesses that you do."

"What weaknesses, Benjamin? Tell me, please! I have done all that has ever been asked—what weaknesses?"

Benjamin smiled and there was a world of sadness in it. "The weaknesses of many a warrior, Matthew. The weakness of many a man, in fact. You see what is before you—you do not often see what is inside. Rachel can and she will." Benjamin smiled, glancing to Zeke, an appraising look in his eyes. "Now this one, he can see inside the soul, quite well. But his body is weak."

Benjamin looked once more at Matthew. "You cannot win a war by might alone. I thought perhaps you understood that. You knew that sacrifices would have to be made."

"Sacrifices," Matthew whispered bitterly, the word like ashes on his tongue. Part of him wanted to move toward Benjamin, wanted to fight, wanted to scream. Rachel, his soft, sweet wife, she wasn't a warrior. She was his woman, his comfort. "Damn you," he rasped, shaking his head. "She isn't a warrior."

Benjamin shook his head. "She had to become one—as did all of you the day this darkness came into this land. Why can you not see that?"

"And this is what my God would have me do? Ask my woman to fight battles?" Matthew raged. "She should be home— *safe.*"

"And ever lonely. Away from you, mourning you, for the rest of her life. For she will never love another, not the way she loves you. Especially now that she has seen you again, now that she knows you live still." Benjamin shook his head. "It isn't just the monsters you must face. You must learn how to make warriors from those they have changed—men and women who will become what you are. You are a warrior and have been from the beginning, Matthew. But Rachel, she was made into one. She knows how to do what you do not. She looks inside a person. And she sees inside the heart. And there's more—so much more."

Matthew clenched hands into angry fists as he stared at Benjamin. "More to what?" he demanded.

Benjamin smiled and obliquely said, "More to her." Without another word, he faded away and was lost to sight.

Chapter Four

She looked better. Much better.

Almost disturbingly so.

Matthew hadn't seen another pale one who had color quite like Rachel had. She looked almost like she had when she was human—a soft flush high on her cheeks, her lips rosy. But her heart rate was far too slow, and she only breathed a few times a minute.

She kept glancing at the horizon with a nervousness in her eyes.

Matthew stayed just at her shoulder, watching her closely as they walked to the cave. Sunrise was still a bit away. They had time. He understood the fear though. He could feel the coming sun himself and he wanted to be deep inside the caves before the sun even neared the horizon...

A wolf-creature.

The smell of the male was unmistakable. The monsters seemed to be in an almost constant state of rut. Heavy in the air, he smelled the scent of fear, excitement and sexual hunger, a miasma that followed the wolf-creatures everywhere they went.

Some of them didn't need the moon to change.

Those were the stronger ones. And the most deadly, it seemed. They changed at will and when they bit a human, the person almost always survived the sickness and come the next moonrise, they changed into a wolf-creature as well.

"Go back to the cave, Rachel," Matthew said flatly. The heavy press of his fangs throbbed in his sockets and his gums itched. His mouth watered, already craving the taste of wolf blood and his heart pounded in anticipation of the coming fight.

It wasn't until he started to head away from Rachel that he realized she hadn't headed back to the cave.

Instead, Rachel stood staring in the direction of the wolf, her head cock, her eyes wide, that odd fey look to them he'd seen earlier.

And she looked almost as hungry now as she had when she'd been following the scent of roasting meat to Ezekiel's home.

"It smells good," she whispered gruffly, her lids drooping.

The smell of fear—*damn it.*

She shook her head, muttering to herself. "Bad man, wicked thing. Shouldn't be allowed out..."

Then she took off running and she moved like the wind, moving past Matthew with a speed that made him feel like he was standing still.

When he did finally catch her, it was because she had stopped. Perhaps stopped wasn't the word. Rachel had launched herself at the wolf-thing and Matthew's heart split in two as he watched her tear it. Fear ate him—Rachel knew nothing of how to fight, but there she was, tearing at the wolf like a woman possessed.

He needed to get her away.

But on the ground, there was a battered, bloodied woman.

The wolf-creature had raped her and she bled all over from a dozen nasty bites. Matthew couldn't stand her screams.

It would take only moments to lull her into sleep and Rachel—he shoved his fear for her aside. She was stronger now.

It would take moments and then whatever wounds the wolf-monster did—

Matthew would have to live with the guilt. He had done this to her. He and he alone. She wouldn't die. The wolf-creature wouldn't kill Rachel easily. Matthew knelt by the screaming woman's side, catching her eyes with his. She stared at him, her torn mouth open, tears streaming down her face.

"Sleep now," he whispered. "Sleep."

The scream cut off abruptly and her face went slack. He was aware of the silence behind him—terror filled him. Rachel was alive. He could hear her heartbeat. She was alive—he would take care of her. Whatever harm had been done to her...

Matthew rose, tensing his body prepared to lunge and instead found himself staring dumbly at Rachel.

The wolf-creature lay on the ground, all but slack with terror. She sat atop him, staring down at him with a solemn face. Her eyes glowed, her mouth gleamed wet in the moonlight and the delicate point of fang showed as she spoke, "You're to die, you understand that."

The wolf-creature just stared at her.

She sighed, shaking her head. "Change back. Do not lay there like some animal when I know some part of you understands me. You know what you did was wrong—I feel that inside you. Change back and face your sentence like a man."

Sentence... Matthew thought, watching her. He started toward her. "Rachel, there's nothing left inside him of the man he was. Just a monster."

She lifted her gaze up. Shaking her head, she murmured, "There is. I feel it, Matthew. Just like I feel that she will not become the foul thing he is. He chose it—he wanted to be a monster. You chose not to become a monster. I chose not to become one. He wanted to be one." Her voice dropped to a ghostly whisper and she repeated it one final time, "He wanted to."

Then she snapped out, "Change *back.*"

Matthew stared, shocked, as the fur slowly receded back into flesh, as the elongated bones shifted and the wolf-man became simply man. A man he knew. His name was Robert. Matthew had known him since they'd been boys—Robert had always been weak-willed. Although Matthew would not have called him evil.

"Robert."

Robert snarled up at him and tried to shove Rachel off. She simply planted her hand in his face and shoved back. "Be silent. Be still," she warned. Lifting her eyes, she stared at Matthew. "We have no fire."

He drew the silver knife he carried at his waist and said, "I will deal with him."

Rachel lifted a brow. "No. This is mine."

"Rachel."

She shook her head. "This is mine. I found him. I judged him—his sentence is mine to carry out." She held out her hand for the knife.

And for some inexplicable reason, Matthew found himself handing it to her. He watched in sheer, dumb shock as she lifted it over head, driving it straight into Robert's heart and the man stared up at her stupefied as the knife flashed down like a silver streak.

Smoke rose from his chest as Rachel slowly and thoroughly twisted the knife, destroying the heart completely.

Slowly, Matthew asked, "What is this talk you speak of...sentences and judgment? Judgment is not ours."

Rachel rose slowly, stepping delicately away from Robert's still body. "No. It is not. But he cannot be allowed to roam among our lands—and what man can stop him? There must be peacemakers—there must be balance. Men cannot find these things. We must. And we will."

Then she looked to the woman laying on the ground, her face crumpling. "Oh, she hurts. She hurts so badly." She moved to the woman and knelt by her side, stroking her hand down hair tangled and matted with blood. "It will be all right, love. I promise you, it will."

Matthew didn't want to add to the grief he saw in Rachel's eyes. How could he explain that within a few weeks, the woman's mind would be eaten up with the madness that came with the moon? She would soon want nothing more than to feed her hungers, both physical and sexual.

"No, she won't."

Matthew started. Rachel gently brushed bits of dirt away from the woman's face. "She has a good heart, a strong soul. That is the heart of a Hunter. The heart of a warrior."

"A Hunter."

The warm golden glow manifested before them as Rachel said quietly, "A Hunter."

Benjamin stepped forward and his eyes darkened with rage as he stared at the woman. He knelt beside her, touching his hands to the nasty bites that marred her flesh. Every place his hands touched, a golden glow was left and when that golden glow faded, only healed flesh remained.

"I cannot take away the memories. The memories are what gives a warrior, a Hunter, her resolve," Benjamin said quietly as he worked. "It would be like if I made you forget your Rachel, Matthew. With nothing to hold on to, perhaps you as well, would have become a monster."

Matthew curled his lip. "So you leave her bitter memories?"

"No. I leave her with the understanding of why she must fight the evil that did this to her, so that another woman might never know it," Benjamin replied levelly.

Benjamin's hands passed over all the injuries that Matthew's eyes could see and then the angel rested his hands low over her belly. Those injuries there must be the worst and he did not want to imagine the pain she suffered. "Although I have dulled her memories some, even if I could completely remove her memory of this night, I would not. It is not my place. Memory is a personal thing—if she is to forget, then she will."

"She shouldn't forget."

Matthew looked at Rachel. Her voice was low, angry and passionate. Tears glimmered in her soft brown eyes and her voice was hoarse with the anger that he sensed within her. "And she won't. There is too much anger and fear inside her. She fears it happening again. She's angry it happened at all. And she's afraid it could happen to another—she has a daughter. Sisters. She'll be one of us."

"You would have her remember this?" Matthew demanded, slashing a hand toward the dead body laying just a few feet away.

Rachel shook her head. "No. I would that it *never* happened. But it did. And now what I want is more people who are strong enough to help Hunt the monsters who would do this. To keep them from doing it before it can happen."

There was something about the way she said it...*Hunt*. Almost like it became a different word entirely. Matthew caught a glimpse of Benjamin from the corner of his eye and he was watching Rachel with approving eyes.

Benjamin flicked Matthew an odd, sidelong glance. "There must be balance, Matthew. Always."

Her name was Mary.

In the cool darkness of the cave, Rachel watched to make sure she continued to sleep before rising and turning to Matthew. He had carried the sleeping woman back here silently and now he just stared at Rachel silently.

What was he thinking?

He looked at her so strangely.

Had ever since he'd come on her to find her rising from that wolf-creature, the thing's blood hot in her mouth. Rachel honestly didn't remember feeding on him. She didn't remember the fiery hot pain as her fangs broke through so fast, didn't remember lunging for him, none of it.

Well, she remembered feeling almost euphorically satisfied. But then the euphoria cleared—like icy water splashed in her face, she realized where she was and what had happened. And too much of what happened. It was no monster that she had fed on. It was a man, and one she knew.

Robert wasn't a man she'd ever particularly cared for, although she wouldn't have thought he'd be a rapist. The flaws inside his character had always been there. But the change he went through brought them out, made them worse. He hadn't been a monster—until he chose to become one.

Matthew stared at her. His dark blue eyes were opaque, unreadable. He didn't know what to make of her, of what had happened.

Rachel sighed, casting a glance over her shoulder at Mary. It had been justice, what she had done. Robert had needed to die. If he hadn't died, then he would have killed again, and again, again and again. Her gut murmured that if Matthew had killed Robert, it would rest easier on his soul, but it bothered him that she had done it.

He looked at her and didn't understand what he saw.

Rachel, though, had never seen so clearly. Destiny wasn't something she understood, but she already accepted it.

Her and her husband's lives lay planned out before them—they had to hunt down the creatures like Robert—save the ones like Mary, ones who'd become the warriors, the Hunters. Kill the monsters. Train the Hunters.

It was all so clear.

She just had to make him see it.

Right now though—she had other plans in mind.

Licking her lips, she gestured to him, leading him past a rock formation that jutted out from the cave wall, hiding them from view. Before Benjamin had left them, he'd said he wanted Mary to rest until her body recovered a little so he had placed her mind into a resting state that would last a day or so.

Right now, she lay sleeping peacefully by the fire, covered with a rough cloth. Rachel had tucked her into one of Matthew's tunics until they could get Mary some clothing.

But Rachel didn't want to make love to her husband in view of another person, whether the woman was asleep or not.

"Rachel—"

She could see the worry in his eyes, the questions, the need to talk. He had questions about what had happened earlier. About what was happening to her, to them, to their lives. She had no answers for him, but Rachel didn't need any.

She had everything she needed right here in front of her.

Lifting a hand, she covered his lips with her fingers. Softly, she murmured, "Hush." She moved against him, rising on her toes as she wrapped one arm around his neck. Her breasts crushed into his chest and she moaned hungrily as his hands came up to cup her hips. "Just touch me—nothing else matters now, does it? We are together, alive, safe. Isn't that all we need?"

So many questions, she could see them lingering in his eyes. "Shhh," she whispered, leaning into him and replacing her fingers with her lips. She licked at his mouth delicately, shivering as his taste flooded her senses.

That taste had always intoxicated her, but it seemed so much *more* now. Everything seemed so much more. Life seemed so much more. The love in her heart seemed so much more. She shivered as he groaned, the vibration of it rumbling against her breasts. Her nipples tightened to the point of pain.

She felt it, the second his control snapped and whatever questions and doubts he had simply faded away. Matthew's arms came around her and he whirled, pressing her against the smooth, cool wall of rock at her back.

His hands shoved the swaths of cloth covering her to her waist as he tore his mouth away from hers, his head moving down her throat. She gasped at the hot sensation of his teeth raking along the sensitive cord of flesh there. "You are right," he rasped. "You are with me—this is all that matters for now."

Between her legs, she felt the hot, thick column of flesh pressing against her then he was inside. Sharp discomfort lanced through her as he pushed inside, deep and fast—but she clung to him with greedy hands. Within moments, she was as wet as he was hard, the slick flesh of her sex clutching at his cock.

"I love you," he muttered, his mouth pressed against her neck. Rachel brought her hand up, pressing his head against her, hungry to feel his mouth on her. "I love you so much—I ached for you, longed for you while slept the daylight away. And I had to force myself to stay away from you through the nights. Do not ever leave me, Rachel."

He thrust against her as he spoke and she arched into him, taking him as hungrily, as desperately as he took her. "I will not, so long as you never leave me," she promised, one hand fisted in his hair, holding him to her. She clutched at his shoulders with her other hand, keeping him as close as she could.

There was a fiery yet icy cold pain at her neck that faded almost as soon as she felt it, replaced by a blissful lassitude. Her eyes flew wide as she realized he had bitten her—the shock of it spurred a new hunger and she screamed, arching her back and bringing up her legs, wrapping them around his waist, her heels digging into his back.

"Matthew!"

He pummeled his hips into the cradle of hers and the power of his thrusts, the iron hard feel of his cock felt almost brutal, yet she craved more. The tension mounted inside her body, building and building, yet she couldn't seem to reach the peak of it, arching against him, clutching at him with desperate hands.

His mouth came up and covered hers, his tongue pushing greedily into her mouth. She caught it in her teeth, biting down lightly and he growled against her. One hand came up, cupping the back of her hair, fisting in the long locks and dragging her head back, staring into her eyes.

His other hand palmed her rump, cupping the taut flesh, kneading it roughly, restlessly. His hand left her for one second and then came down quickly, swiftly, striking her flesh in a light smack. Rachel stiffened against him and in that brief moment, everything inside exploded.

She stiffened around the thick pillar of his sex even as he shoved inside her, screaming hoarsely as she came, her body quaking in his arms, jerking with violent spasms.

Rachel stared at him for a long moment and then her vision started to gray.

Matthew watched as her lashes fluttered down, dimly aware of it, but the monstrous lust inside rode him still and he moved within her, gathering her body close. Burying his face against her neck, he growled as her pussy continued to ripple and spasm around his cock.

Those tiny little caresses drove him to insanity, pushing him over the edge. His cock jerked and he came inside her, the intensity of it leaving him weak. He sank to his knees, still holding her trembling body in his arms.

His entire body felt like mush.

His brain had ceased to function.

Each slow beat of his heart echoed throughout his entire being and the scent of his wife's body flooded his senses. For a very long while, everything but the two of them ceased to exist.

But then he became aware of the sweet taste of blood that still lingered in his mouth, the faint scent of it that still lingered in the air.

"My God," he whispered, lifting his head to stare down at Rachel. "What have I done?"

Her lashes lifted slowly and she smiled sleepily up at him. "Hummm?"

"Rachel..."

She arched against him like a little kitten, wrapping her arms around his neck and cuddling close. "You think too much, Matthew. You have done nothing wrong. I am not hurt. You are not hurt. Let us just rest—we have so much work ahead of us. You shouldn't weary yourself fighting with your own conscious."

Matthew was waiting when Mary's eyes opened late that evening. It wasn't that he didn't trust his wife.

But she hadn't seen these creatures as the wolf's change started to come on them. Matthew had. It could come suddenly—or it could wait until the coming of the full moon.

But Matthew wouldn't risk this woman rising from her sleep alone.

If there was already a monster lurking inside her soul, he would have to deal with it.

Just as well that Rachel had wandered out of the cave the moment the sun set. If he had to kill this woman, it would weigh heavy on his soul, but it would be easier if Rachel weren't there to witness it.

A sigh escaped Mary just before her lashes lifted.

"Hello, Mary," he said quietly.

She stiffened at the sound of his voice, her entire body tensing.

Matthew remained where he was, waiting until she sought him out in the dark. She sat up, scrambling back away from him, her eyes half-wild as she stared at him. "Wuh—where am I?" she demanded, her voice cracking. Her eyes darted around the darkness of the cave, and Matthew knew she wouldn't see much to reassure her.

"You're safe."

She laughed brokenly. "I'm not safe! That thing—he—what he did, how can I be safe? How can any of us, while monsters like that exist?" She lifted her hands, staring down at them.

Matthew watched, unsure of what to do, as she closed her hands into fists. "How can you fight things like that? He was so strong..." Her voice faded away and she lifted her eyes, looking at him. A lone tear trickled down her face as she asked, "How can you fight that?"

Behind him, Rachel slid out of the shadows. "We fight them. Men and women alone cannot, Mary. They haven't the strength—they simply become helpless victims like you were."

"Rachel—" Matthew moved to catch her, wondering where in the hell she had come from. She slipped past him, evading him as she moved to stand in front of him.

Rachel stood before Mary. "You're not helpless anymore, Mary. You do not have to be a victim anymore."

The tears gleaming in Mary's eyes made them flash. Her mouth quivered.

Rachel reached out a hand to the woman and Matthew watched as Mary reached out, not for Rachel's hand, but for Rachel, wrapping her arms around Rachel in a desperate embrace as sobs started to tear from her. Mary sank to her knees and Rachel just stood there, stroking her hand down Mary's hair, murmuring softly to her.

The moments stretched out as Mary cried, until the sobs turned hoarse and eventually lost sound and still the woman's body shook and trembled with the force of her crying. Finally, she stilled and fell back on her heels, then to her bottom, covering her face with her hands.

Matthew circled around them, not daring to move close as Rachel knelt in front of Mary, gazing at her with searching eyes. "What is it you want?"

Mary swallowed, her hands falling to rest in her lap. She lifted a face red and swollen from crying to look at Rachel. "I'm not strong enough," she rasped out. "For what I want."

"Are you so certain?"

A strong warrior, your woman... Benjamin murmured to him. The soft, comforting voice once more whispered only in Matthew's mind. From the intent look on Rachel's face as she studied Mary, she was unaware of the angel's presence. "I didn't want this for her."

Neither did she. But it is the path that lies before you both now—and for Mary as well. And many, many others...

"What are we to do?" Matthew whispered.

Find them. That will be the easy part. The hard part is everything else...like what you saw last night. And it's only beginning.

Epilogue

She hadn't aged.

Matthew watched as she stood in the shadows of a great stone chamber, her eyes watching the proceedings before her with calm, measuring eyes. Little caused emotion on her face after all this time.

There was emotion there, though. Matthew felt the echoes of what tore through her heart inside his own. She'd turned to him in the night for comfort—they'd turn to each other. After so much time, they still had each other.

The witch that stood before them now was young, full of anger, full of rage. Her name was Agnes. Matthew looked at the young, delicate looking thing and felt his heart break.

Her destiny, just like his own, just like Rachel's, lay before her. But Agnes' would be a long, painful one, he suspected. There was anger and rage and suffering in her heart.

What they had done...

"There will be no judgment."

Matthew was pleased with the decision, although years had passed since Rachel and he had left the Council. These decisions were no longer theirs to make, but the men making them were good men. One, in particular, had all of Matthew's faith.

Malachi was an old one, a powerful one. It had taken all of Rachel's charm to convince that bastard into the realm of the

Hunters, but she had done it. Matthew hadn't doubted her. In the past nine hundred years, she accomplished things that no mortal being should be able to accomplish...mortal.

He smiled as the word circled through his mind.

The men and women of the Hunter's Council, they didn't realize it, but they were still mortal. Just much longer lived than the humans they fought so hard to protect. All of them would die—even Matthew, even Rachel.

Some would die of old age.

Some of would die in a blaze of glory as they fought this fight.

And some might even do as so many others that Rachel and Matthew had known—they might take their own lives when the years stretched on too long and the loneliness grew too great. Matthew knew the Lord above was merciful—Matthew only hoped He would have compassion on those poor souls.

But all of the Hunters would die—none of them were the immortal creatures they had come to believe. Some would go more peacefully than others. But all would go into the waiting arms of God.

It was just a matter of when.

The end...
Actually...it's more like...the beginning

Hunter's Pride

Prologue

Pride Mountain...for as long as any of them could remember, Pride Mountain had been theirs. Not all of them stayed there, but even those who left, they knew Pride Mountain was home.

It wasn't a true mountain, more of a big hill, but for Michigan, it seemed plenty mountainous enough. And it was theirs...the mountain itself and the land that stretched around for it for miles.

It had been for years, going back nearly two centuries, almost since the first time people settled in the region.

They didn't like change.

Change could be dangerous—that was one thing none of them ever forgot. Change could bring predators into their midst, for the sake of fame and notoriety, for the sake of fortune...or for the sake of mayhem.

But it hadn't been *them* that had brought this latest change.

He scented it first, the powerful sour scent of fear. The moonlight filtered down through the canopy of leaves as he wove silently through the trees. Fear, sweat, blood...somebody was hurt. Scared.

She was running—he could hear branches snapping, her harsh ragged breathing. A soft cry when she fell. Leaves crunched as she pushed herself back up to her feet.

Soft, desperate little sobs. Those cries barely even sounded human. More like an animal weak and terrified, soft little whimpers and mewls that sounded disturbingly like the plaintive cries of a cougar's young. He knew when the others became aware of her.

Suddenly, he wasn't alone as he moved closer to the source of the disturbance.

"Son?"

He glanced over his shoulder at his dad. Although he was nearly as tall as his father, he had yet to fill out much. At nineteen, he stood nearly six three and was as lanky as a scarecrow. But he was strong. He knew how to hunt, how to fight.

How to protect.

That was his job. It was *their* job and they took it seriously.

Protect—

There was somebody else. Somebody chasing her. He stank—reeked of blood and violence.

"She's hurt," he said, his voice barely a whisper. "I smell blood. He's chasing her."

Nausea roiled through him as he scented something else. Lust. It was like a fever boiling in the man's blood.

His father breathed deeply, his eyes darkening as he murmured, "Yes, I know. Go back to the others. We'll handle this."

We...his father, Ryan Pride, and the three men that served under him. Not a king, exactly, but definitely the leader. And Duncan would one day take his place.

"No." Shaking his head, Duncan turned his eyes back in the direction of the disturbing scents of blood, fear, and violence. Blood, he was used to. After all, they had come up Pride Mountain on this moonlit night to hunt. But he couldn't ever recall smelling such fear.

"Duncan, now."

"No, Dad." He shook his head a second time. "I found her. I have to help her."

It was long standing custom—the one who caught the scent of the prey led the kill. But it wasn't so much the kill he wanted, not yet. It was the need to protect.

Behind him, he heard his father's quiet sigh, sensed his frustration. He had to do this, though...she needed him.

She could hear him behind her.

She had his blood on her hands and it felt like it was burning her. She hurt inside—her legs pulled with every step and running was agony.

Kennedy tripped, falling down. Rocks tore into her knees, cutting her flesh. She cried out and then clamped her hand over her mouth.

No, he couldn't hear her. Couldn't catch her.

If he did...*Oh, God*...she prayed silently.

With every muscle in her body screaming, she shoved herself to her feet. A desperate energy flooded her and she took off running once more.

Kennedy didn't know where she was—she'd been running for so long and it was so damned dark. But she couldn't stop.

"Found you, bitch!"

Glancing over her shoulder, she saw him. Her stepfather's face was smeared with blood, and the ugly gash on the left side of his face had dried over.

Part of her wished she still had the poker she had hit him with. *Should have brought it with me...*

"Little bitch, you're going to pay for that," he said, his voice cold and angry. He didn't even sound winded—

With a sob, she forced her legs to move faster, run harder.

And when his hand closed around the back of her neck, she screamed.

Seconds later, she was on the ground, her face pressed into the dirt. He still had his hand on the back of her neck and she could hardly breathe. Her hands tore and dug into the earth as she tried to get away from him.

He laughed. "No way, you little slut," he said as he levered himself over her.

Against the naked curve of her rump, she could feel him as he wedged himself against her.

No...not again!

Squeezing her eyes shut, she tried to block it out.

Block it all out.

None of this had happened—she hadn't gone home yet, he hadn't grabbed her...she was out with friends and they were laughing...

Laughing...

Screaming...

His hands fell away and he swore softly. Freed, she shoved her body upright and tried to crawl away. Her limbs didn't want to work, but she dragged herself a few feet away.

Just as she fell against the trunk of a tree, she heard it again.

That scream...it wasn't human.

It was a deep, terrifying scream, unlike anything she'd ever heard before.

"She saw us."

Duncan sat on the ground, the girl's head pillowed on his lap as he stroked her tangled hair back from her battered face.

Glancing up at his father, he said, "She saw cats, Dad. That's all."

Big cats. But they weren't cougars. Duncan and the others were much, *much* bigger than a cougar. But they had been seen once or twice before and they *looked* like cougars.

His voice was hoarse and ragged as he whispered, "He raped her, Dad."

They knew the man. Knew he had a violent streak in him. They watched him, but other than bar room brawls, there hadn't been much trouble with the bastard.

Until now.

Zane Matthews spoke up, his voice harsh and angry as he looked at Kennedy. "Where do you think her mom is?"

"Where she usually is," Ryan said bleakly. "Out screwing around. Masters here finally snapped, I guess."

Kelly and Jack Masters had been married for close to ten years, but that hadn't stopped Kelly from screwing any man she could get close to. Hell, Duncan was nearly twenty years younger than her and she hadn't been at all subtle when she'd tried to come on to him last year.

She stank of other men, cigarette smoke, whiskey, and easy sex. Even the thought of touching her had turned his stomach.

Now he wished he had, though. Touched her and torn her apart. He knew, as well as he knew his own name, that Kelly Masters was part of the reason her daughter lay half naked on the wooded hillside of Pride Mountain.

Jack Masters had lost it, all right. And his stepdaughter had paid for it. Adopted daughter...he thought absently. Jack had adopted Kennedy years ago.

She was so tiny—rage burned low in his belly as he recalled just how tiny she had looked, curled on the ground as Jack pushed himself to his feet, dragging his jeans back up as he faced Duncan down.

"If you want a piece of the little whore, go ahead," Jack had said, his voice wary. Jack's eyes had been glowing, a sure sign of anger and fear. The glow had only increased as Duncan moved closer.

"You're dead, Masters," Duncan had told him quietly.

And he was.

Duncan had killed him. He could still feel the blood on his claws...hands. His hands...he had Changed back to his human form just before he'd ripped Jack's heart from his body. Jack had shifted to his own preferred form, one that was half man, half wolf. He'd known he was fighting for his life and he'd fought hard.

But Duncan couldn't feel anything from the various bruises, bites, and claw marks on his body. They didn't matter.

None of it mattered.

"We need to get her into town...*before* she wakes up," Zane said quietly as he padded back into the clearing.

"Masters?" Ryan asked.

Zane said, "Hidden for now. We'll burn him later. But for now..."

Ryan nodded, hunkering down in front of Duncan. "You need to let me have her, son. She needs to get to the hospital."

Duncan cradled her protectively against his chest. "I'll do it."

Ryan shook his head. "Look at yourself, boy. You're torn up and bleeding all over. We're going to have enough questions—we can't risk anybody seeing you until you've healed up."

And that would take a few more hours. Dropping his eyes, he studied her battered face. "What's going to happen to her?"

With a sigh, Ryan said, "I don't know. But he can't touch her again. And for now, that's enough."

Chapter One

Little whore—just like your mama.

It was a dream. Kennedy knew that.

But she couldn't push it aside. Couldn't wake up.

In the dream, she was fourteen, rooting through her closet for something to wear to the party.

Jack came in—she smelled the liquor on him even before she heard him.

Little whore...

He stared at Kennedy as she stood there wearing just the bright red button down. *She ain't here—out fucking anybody she can find.*

Her mother. Yeah, Kennedy knew what her mother was. She pretended otherwise, but she knew. Hard not to when the woman would come home drunk, her clothes messed up, makeup all smeared.

You think you're going to go out and leave me here, too? Jack stared at her, his eyes on her bare legs, and Kennedy circled away from him, grabbing the jeans on her bed.

He laughed. And then he reached for her.

She ran, but she only made it to the living room before he caught her. Toyed with her.

Things turned into a blurry, pain-filled haze and in her sleep, Kendall sobbed.

His weight was suffocating her and when he finally moved away, for a moment, she couldn't do anything but suck air into desperate lungs. *You just stay right there, little cunt. I'm not done with you...*

No. Kendall shook her head silently, watching him as he turned to grab the beer bottle from the coffee table. Scuttling back on her hands and knees, she moved away. When she came up against the wall, she pushed herself to her feet, trying to convince herself to run.

But she *hurt...*

Didn't I tell you to stay there? Little bitch—your mama might not listen to me... yet...but you are going to. Get back where you were.

Kennedy shook her head, folding her arms around her middle and staring at him. Jack moved towards her and she snapped. The poker was in her hand before she realized it and she swung at him like she was going for a homerun in softball practice.

He fell to the floor like a stone and she dropped the poker.

And ran. Out the back yard and over the small creek that separated their land from the sprawling forest. Into the woods, heading away from town—into the hills. Pride Mountain—even though it was really nothing more than a big hill, it had been called Pride Mountain for as long as anybody could remember.

She'd run. Just keep running. That was all that mattered.

But he caught her. Dirt and leaves choked her as he pressed her into the ground. *You're going to pay for that...*

She knew. He'd rape her again, maybe even kill her. She wanted to scream, tried to, but with her face pressed into the dirt, she didn't have the breath.

But something did...*something* screamed.

The last thing she could remember clearly was a cat. Not a fuzzy little house cat, either. But a huge, golden cat that looked like something from National Geographic.

And a monster—one with Jack Masters's cruel, cold eyes.

⬥⬥⬥⬥⬥⬥

She woke up with a start. Tears were drying on her face and the pillow was damp. Kennedy shivered, pulling the blankets tighter around her.

"Just a dream," she told herself.

But it wasn't. It had been more than that.

It had actually happened.

Fifteen years ago, her stepfather had raped her. She'd run away and he'd followed her. What had happened then, she didn't know. But Jack Masters was never seen again.

She suspected a lot of people thought she might have killed him and blocked it from her mind. Hell, her own mother had screamed it at her. *You killed him—little whore...you always wanted what was mine.*

Kelly had screamed that at the hospital two days after it had happened. Most of what had happened was a blur. Kennedy remembered the rape with brutal clarity. Remembered running. Falling. Him on top of her—but he didn't rape again.

There had been something there...

Something had saved her.

Images of big cats haunted her dreams.

She was taken out of her mother's custody even before the doctors let her leave the hospital. Lisa and Cole Franklin had taken her—nice people, her foster parents. They'd done everything they could for.

Kennedy had spent the next eight years in their house. They'd gotten her into counseling—and Kennedy knew it had probably helped. They'd kept her mother away from her.

And...they had left her their house.

The childless couple had been killed in a car wreck just three weeks ago. Kennedy still couldn't believe they were gone.

The kind people who had paid her way through college, who had bought her a car when she turned sixteen—the people who had loved her were gone.

Closing her eyes, she swallowed down the sobs as she reached up and touched the string of pearls around her neck. They'd given the necklace to her when she graduated college. There was a matching pair of earrings that had been a present when she graduated high school.

They'd given her so much—and now they were gone.

The Franklins had been the only thing that had brought her back to the small Michigan town where she'd grown up. After graduating from college, Kennedy had found a job as a social worker in Detroit, helping kids get away before they could be hurt like she'd been.

It had been more therapy.

Until the last case.

Marisa Armstrong had been raped, just like Kennedy had been, by her stepfather. Mama had been too busy partying to care. Even when Marisa had hung herself, the bitch had been more worried about her own life and how badly this messed up her fun.

Kennedy hadn't been able to save Marisa.

And that had broken her.

She had been thinking about quitting—Kennedy couldn't take any more, she knew it.

But then the Franklins had died.

They'd died—and they had left everything to her. They'd left her the house and the small bookstore. But Kennedy would rather have them than all the houses and bookstores in the world.

No way to trade, though. They were gone and Kennedy owned the house and the small bookstore Lisa had owned.

At least for a while.

As much as Kennedy had loved her foster parents, as much as she missed them, she didn't know if she could stay in Pride, Michigan.

With a sigh, she climbed from the bed, gazing around her old room with bleak eyes.

It hadn't changed.

The pale blue walls, the lace eyelet curtains, the pictures of old school friends, and brightly colored posters. On the dresser there was a framed picture of her with Lisa and Cole the day she'd graduated from high school.

Even though she couldn't see it well in the early morning light, she knew how it looked.

How she had looked. Almost happy.

Kennedy forced herself to climb from the bed and move across the room into the bathroom. She turned on the shower spray, knowing it would take a few minutes to heat up and in the meantime, she left to gather some clothes from the suitcase she had yet to unpack.

Five minutes later, she was under the hot pulsating spray, trying desperately not think.

If she could avoid thinking, maybe she could avoid remembering.

The time would come when she would have to think—Kennedy knew that.

She'd come back to Pride for a reason.

Not for her mother, and not to try to accept what the woman had let happen to her only daughter. She'd accepted that.

A long time ago.

But it wasn't enough.

She had to know who had saved her.

Duncan Pride stood in the doorway of *A Page Apart,* staring at the woman at the register. She was bent over a book, studying the page intently. Her hair, dark and wild, spiraled down around her shoulders in riotous waves. As he continued to debate going inside, she started to twine one fat curl around her finger.

He'd known the Franklins would leave the bookstore to Kennedy. Although her mother hadn't ever let them adopt her, Kennedy had belonged more to Lisa and Cole than the cold bitch who birthed her. One of things she'd done on her own after she turned eighteen, she'd changed her name.

Kennedy Franklin, no longer Kennedy Masters.

Duncan hadn't been sure what to expect. He'd seen her around town a few times after that night. For a while, she'd had been scared of her own shadow.

Then fall came and Duncan had left again for college. He rarely saw her after that. And not at all for more than seven years. She saw the Franklins often, but they always traveled to see her in Detroit. She rarely came home.

Not that Duncan could blame her.

Pride, Michigan was his home—had been home to his family for nearly two hundred years. They'd come here seeking solitude. They stayed because it was home.

The nightmares he had of what had happened to her were nothing compared to what he imagined she experienced. What Jack Masters had done to his stepdaughter was the worst that had ever happened in Pride, at least in recent memory.

People forgot. Within a few months, people had acted normally around her again. But Duncan couldn't forget—all he could remember was how frail, how small she had been as he held her. Every bruise he'd seen was imprinted on his memory. Every streak of blood.

So how in the hell could he walk in there and act normal? She hardly knew him.

Just leave...

She wouldn't even remember him. They'd only seen each other in passing, and not even that for years.

But before Duncan could convince himself to turn around and walk, she looked up. Through the glass, he met her brown eyes and he forced a smile as he opened the door and stepped inside.

Too late now...

"Hello, Kennedy."

She studied him for a minute with curious eyes. Finally, a smile curled her lips upward just a little. "Duncan Pride." Her eyes dropped the badge he wore clipped to his belt and she arched a brow. "Like father, like son?" she asked.

Duncan shrugged. "Seemed like the right choice," he murmured.

"How is your father?"

He glanced away. "Died a few years ago."

She paled. "I'm sorry, Duncan."

He nodded a little. "Happened fast. That's all you can really hope for." Well, except for more time, he guessed.

She was quiet for a moment, but he could see the questions in her eyes. "Shot in the line of duty," he said softly. "Somebody from out of town was accused of attacking a local girl. He went to the hotel to question him and the guy tried to run, pulled a gun on Dad. They both got shots off—both of them died."

He didn't elaborate more than that. Wasn't much else he could say—how could he explain to a mortal that his father was shot facing down a feral werewolf that thought he could make Pride his personal hunting grounds? In more ways than one. It was suspected that the werewolf was responsible for two missing people, plus it looked like he had attacked several different women, not just the one who initially came forward.

If the bastard had been a mortal, Ryan Pride would still be alive. He'd been shot at point blank range, but a shapeshifter could heal almost any wound. But not one inflicted by a silver bullet, a silver bullet shot straight into the heart. Fortunately, the sheriff had known he was going after a non-mortal and he'd been prepared. He'd used silver ammo as well.

Both were dead and the Prides had fulfilled their duties.

Duty—one of the things that kept the Prides here. Oh, some left, but many of them stayed. They'd been charged with protecting these lands and it was a responsibility they took seriously.

A duty given to them by the Council.

The Council...he'd been approached by them while he was at college. Not a big surprise, sooner or later most of the Prides had been approached. Some had gone to serve that honored organization. Some chose to try to live a life as normal as possible. Others came home.

Duncan had come home. When he was a kid, he had dreams of being a Hunter. His dad had told him of his responsibilities early on. He was his father's only son, the one that Pride Mountain would pass to, and hopefully, Duncan would take over for his father as leader of the Pride. But Ryan had understood what it was like to have dreams—dreams of something exciting.

If Duncan had chosen to join the Hunters instead, Ryan would have accepted that, happily and with a lot of pride.

Duncan had declined the offer, though, to join the Hunters. In a way, he already served the Council.

Nearly a hundred and fifty years ago, the Council had sent an emissary to Pride Mountain. It had been Duncan's great grandfather who had led the Pride then. When he was given charge of these lands, he had done so willingly.

For as long as the Prides handled the problems that arose with feral vamps and shifters, no Hunter would be sent to claim land anywhere near their home.

That could have gotten...dicey, to say the least. Paranormal creatures were notoriously territorial and the lands in Pride, Michigan had been in the Pride family for more than two hundred years, even before Michigan became a state. They wouldn't have easily moved aside if a Hunter had felt called to their lands.

Especially since chances are it would have been another shifter. This far north in Michigan, the extremes in day and night weren't that easy for a lot of Hunters. Something in the air really bothered the witches—it was suspected it had something to do with the magnetic fields. A witch had to be born in the far north, used to the effects the magnetic fields had on their powers, otherwise, it took quite a while to acclimate. Their powers were a bit harder to control. Some became noticeably stronger, which required more training. Others lost some power.

Neither one was something a lot of witches liked.

Witches really liked keeping things as level as they could. From what Duncan could tell from the witches he had met, they were damned near control freaks. Having Mother Nature wreak havoc on their gifts was probably a pain in the ass.

More, it wasn't just the witches that didn't like the adjustment. The longer days in the summer kept the vampires too constrained. The werewolves had the opposite problem—the nights were difficult in the winter, especially when the moon rode high in the sky. So they never stayed too long.

The only ones that weren't affected this far in the north were the natural shapeshifters, ones like the members of the Pride. Shifters who didn't rely on the cycles of the moon to harness the power to Change.

So it would have been a shifter, either a wolf or another feline that came and settled if the Pride hadn't accepted to guard the lands.

Up until Ryan had been killed by the feral werewolf, it had been a sacrifice that had come with little cost.

"I hate to hear that."

Kennedy's soft voice pulled Duncan out of the well of memories and he looked up at her with a faint smile. "Dad loved his job, loved what he did."

"He was a good man. A brave one. A kind one." Her eyes moved away but not before he saw them darken from memory.

Ryan had been at her side when she woke in the hospital. It had been Ryan who intervened when her mother tried to literally drag her out of the hospital.

Her memories of Ryan Pride were probably not very good ones.

Duncan forced a smile and said, "Yes. He was. I hear you're planning on moving back to Pride, at least for a while."

She shrugged. "Yes. Not sure how long."

"We don't really have much need for social workers. There's only four of them in the county, and one of them is part time."

Kennedy smiled, flashing a dimple in her cheek. "That's a good thing. I'm getting out of social work." Even though she smiled, he saw the sadness in her eyes. Something had happened.

Nodding, he said, "Understandable. I imagine it's a hell of a lot harder in Detroit. So you're going to try running the bookstore, instead?"

One shoulder lifted in a shrug. "Yeah—*try* being the operative word. But Leslie has said she's staying on. Hopefully she can keep me from messing up." She tucked a strand of hair behind her ear and closed her book. "Is there anything you were looking for? Or doing the welcome wagon thing?"

"Both. I'd ordered some books..." He moved to the counter, trying to remember the titles, but she was already turning around.

He braced his elbows on the counter, watching as she flipped through the marked books on the shelves behind the counter. She said something else, but it barely registered.

Duncan was a little too preoccupied with the book on the counter. The one Kennedy had been reading. *Return of the Big Cats to Michigan.*

He'd read it—the natural cougars were an interest of his. It was more of an educational piece, written by a professor in Saginaw. And it detailed the return of the cougars to the state.

Odd reading...

Whoa...

When Duncan Pride left, the bookstore seemed a hell of a lot bigger. There was something almost overwhelming about him. She hadn't seen him in years, and she hadn't ever really talked to him.

He looked a lot like his father.

Both of them had been tall, lean hipped, wide shouldered, with a long, wiry build. Duncan wore his hair a lot longer than his father had. Freed from that stubby ponytail, she imagined the black locks would fall loose to his shoulders.

Duncan's skin was a warm, tawny gold. And odd eyes—almost reflective. Light yellowish brown.

Frowning, she looked back at the book on the counter and opened it, flipping to photographs in the middle. The glossy stills showed images of cougars and the one she liked the most was a face shot. It looked like the photographer had been standing close enough to touch, so close she could see the detail of the black markings on the cat's ears.

And his eyes.

An odd, yellowish brown, nearly the same color as his coat. The same color as Duncan's.

"Huh," she murmured, rubbing her finger across the picture.

Kennedy was pretty sure she hadn't ever seen eyes like that before. Well, not in a person.

The phone rang and absently, she picked it up and said, "*A Page Apart.*" Finally, after three days, she was answering the phone like this place was a business, not her home.

"Hi, Ms. Franklin?"

"Yes."

"This is Casey Matthews—my dad said you were trying to find a guide. Wanted to take some pictures?"

Her first plan for finding more about the cats was just trying to find where their territory was. She wasn't about to ask the Pride family if she could start on their land—not yet. She'd been gone a long time, and what interest did a social worker have in wild cats?

Until she figured out how to handle that dilemma, she was settling for the State Park that bordered the land belonging to the Prides.

"When were you wanting to go? And what were you looking for?"

She feigned curiosity, explained she had always had an interest in photography. *That* at least was the truth, but curiosity didn't quite touch her fascination with cougars.

"I suppose I can guide you to some pretty spots..."

That would work—for now. "I'm probably going to want to do this a few times. Will you be able to help?"

The girl on the other end of the line agreed and Kennedy said a silent *thank you*. Within ten minutes, they had agreed to a date and place to meet and Casey advised Kennedy on what to wear.

She had one week. Kennedy would rather have hooked up a little sooner, but she wasn't going to complain. Nobody else would understand this urgency.

Besides, a week would give her enough time to unpack her camera equipment and hopefully get a hand on some decent hiking gear. Geez...it had been nearly ten years since she had done any serious hiking.

She glanced out the window to the sporting store across the street. It looked like she was going to have to make a trip to *All Outdoors.*

⬛⬛⬛⬛⬛

Casey hung up the phone and looked at her dad. "She just wants to take some pictures. We're going to the state park."

"In a week," Zane said, arching a brow.

The nineteen year old nodded. "Yes, sir. She tried for this weekend but..." She trailed off and shrugged, smiling a little.

This weekend was the full moon. All of them were natural shifters, inheriting the trait through the bloodline, but still, they did feel some strange calling from the moon when it was full. It wasn't an urge they couldn't ignore. None of them *had* to Change with the rising of the full moon.

But they did have to shift occasionally—it was a need. The full moon was as good a night as any. They gathered on Pride Mountain and went hunting.

Even though Zane knew Casey would get Kennedy Franklin gone before nightfall, it was a wise choice. People couldn't always control everything that happened—so why tempt fate?

"She didn't say anything...odd, did she?"

Casey stared at him and he saw the echo of his belated wife in that stare. That look all women seemed to have, when men were acting like idiots. That look that said, *You're so dumb.*

"Exactly what kind of odd do you mean? A lot of people like to hike, Dad."

Zane scowled at his daughter and turned away. Passing a hand over his closely cropped hair, he muttered under his breath. Okay, so there was really nothing for him to worry about. It wasn't like Kennedy Franklin had said, *I want to try to find these big cats that saved me fifteen years ago.*

She had been unconscious through most of it, and terrified for the brief seconds she had seen them. Ryan had been the one to take her report and she didn't remember most of her attack. No reason for her to remember now.

He left without a word and knew that Casey was shaking her head as she watched him walk away.

Yeah, he worried too much. But that was his job.

Chapter Two

Kennedy finished lacing up her hiking boots and cast a look at the clock. It had been more than a month since she had first gone hiking through the State Park. A month of listening to Casey Matthews drone one and one about local flora and fauna. Any time she tried to ask about cougars, the girl managed to successfully, and subtly, redirect the subject.

A lot of people still didn't think there were any more than a couple of cougars, even though science had proved otherwise.

Kennedy had seen the signs of the big cats. A few faint tracks, scat, nothing major. Certainly no sign of cats as big as the ones Kennedy had seen. And Casey never took her to exactly the same place, and more often than not, they ended up on the far side of where Kennedy wanted to look.

So today, Kennedy was going out on her own. She'd checked and double-checked the maps and was pretty certain one of the trails would lead her close to the edge of the state owned land. She planned on marking her own trail and all she was going to do was investigate a little more carefully along that border.

If she found something, she'd decide what to do then.

Her pack sat ready by the door. A couple of nutritional shakes were tucked inside, although she was leaving a small cooler in the truck with sandwiches and soft drinks inside. She had a bottle of water, her camera, and a long flexible walking stick she'd bought when she got her hiking boots.

Kennedy refused to think of *what* she would do if she managed to find some sign of the bigger cats. She'd cross that bridge when she came to it.

Four hours later, Kennedy decided she had definitely made an error in judgment here. She'd gotten lost and had no idea where she was. The trails in this part of the park were steeper and her thighs were screaming from the strain of climbing up and down. Worse, when she'd left the trail behind nearly an hour ago, she had marked the spot. She *knew* she had, but now she couldn't find any of her markers. The bright yellow tags should have stood out easily, but if she had wandered too far from the last one...

Exhausted, she rested her back against a huge pine, breathing in the familiar woodsy scent, and tried to calm the nerves jumping in her belly.

"Now what?" she muttered wearily.

She took a sip from her water bottle and let the tepid water ease her dry throat. There was still a half bottle left, but considering she had really gotten herself turned around, she needed to conserve it. She might be here a while.

They'd find her truck. The park rangers always checked the parking lots at nightfall when the park was scheduled to close and when they found her truck, and not *her* nearby, they'd come looking for her, right?

So do I just stay here? she wondered. But the inactivity after about an hour nearly drove her nuts.

Shoving to her feet, Kennedy continued to trudge through the woods, looking for some sign of a trail.

Zane and Duncan stood staring at the shiny black truck, their expressions grim. The light of the full moon shone brightly down on them and Duncan swore viciously. This had been one hell of a month and he *needed* the release he'd get from a good night of roaming the woods in his other form.

Not just the hunting, although he loved that. He needed the release that came from shifting but it didn't look like he'd get to spend a night wearing anything other than his human skin.

"It's Kennedy Franklin's truck," Zane said unnecessarily.

Sliding Zane a narrow look, Duncan replied testily, "I know that."

He also knew that Kennedy had been spending quite a bit of her time in the forest, hiking the trails, snapping pictures.

She also asked a lot of questions about cougars. Casey had assured both Zane and Duncan that Kennedy hadn't ever seemed interested in anything more than the natural cougars that had slowly started to repopulate the wooded areas of Michigan, but it was enough to set the Pride's nerves on edge.

And now on a full moon, their one night to hunt, she was out there in the woods somewhere. Scowling, he scented the air as he paced the parking lot. To the east. About a mile and half of trail and forestland separated the parking lot from Pride lands. And that was where she had gone.

"Damn it all to hell," he muttered, shaking his head.

"Tell me about it," Zane said.

A new voice joined in on the conversation as Glenna McGuire came walking up. "I've called a couple of our people from Search and Rescue. And Casey got a hold of all the rest. Everybody knows the hunt is off for the night. Nick and Marie will be out here within a half and hour and we can start looking for her."

At least it had been Glenna that found the truck. That wasn't chance, either. She'd taken this job specifically so that they could make sure the park was emptied out on hunt night. Up until now, the only thing she'd had to do was chase out teens who came to the park to make out.

Oh, they'd had hikers get lost before. It was a big park and a popular one, but they hadn't had the bad luck to lose a hiker on hunt night.

And Duncan couldn't get rid of this niggling feeling—she wasn't just out hiking.

Kennedy was looking for something.

Or someone.

"You're sure the word got out to everybody?" he asked tersely.

Glenna lowered her head slightly, a simple gesture of deference. "Casey said she got messages to all of the family."

"What about the twins? Did they get a message or did somebody actually talk to them?"

Behind him, Zane groaned. "Now wouldn't that just be perfect..."

Duncan glanced at him, jaw clenched. "Yeah, wouldn't it?" Jerking his phone from his belt, he accessed the phone number for Douglas and Deacon McGuire, Glenna's first cousins. They were related to Duncan and Zane loosely, cousins several time removed.

They were also eighteen and raging bundles of hormones and hungers. The Change usually hit right when puberty was hitting, sometimes a little later in the males. And the first few Changes were spent in solitude, with nobody but parents on hand to make sure the young shifter was in control.

Douglas and Deacon had been hit hard with the Change, a little late for their kind, just last summer. Ever since, they'd been like live wires, growing a good foot in a year, going from quiet, polite boys to young men that loved nothing more than a good fight, a fast car, and pretty girls.

They were good kids, Duncan knew, but they were wild. When Barbara answered the phone, he could tell by the tone of voice there was a problem.

"They aren't there, are they?" Duncan asked flatly.

Barbara McGuire said shakily, "No. I've been trying to call them, but if they've already hit the hunting grounds...Duncan, they wouldn't hurt anybody."

Duncan really wished he could be so sure. That was why the Pride hunted together, to give the young ones a time to adjust to their fledging abilities without risking anybody getting hurt. "Don't worry about it," he said quietly, hoping his voice wasn't as easy to read as hers was. "We'll find them."

"The hiker that's missing, has he shown up yet?" Barbara asked.

"It's a woman. And no. I have to go—we need to find her." *Before* the twins did. If she saw the two cougars, already bigger than the natural cougars, she'd panic. Panicking around predators was bad.

Very bad.

He met Glenna's eyes as he hung up his phone. "You stay here until Nick and Maria get here. When they get here, you three split up. We don't come in until we find her. And if you run into the twins, call for me."

He met Zane's eyes and gestured toward the forest with a jerk of his head. "Let's go."

* * *

Ooooohhhhh

Kennedy awoke with a whimper, reaching up and pressing a careful hand to her head. It came away sticky. "Not good," she muttered. Slowly, she stretched the rest of her body, taking stock. She bit back a cry when her ankle screamed in agony. Twisted at the least, possibly broken.

Bright moonlight filtered down through the canopy of the trees, casting enough silvery light that she could see up the slope she'd fallen down. As she pushed upright, she twisted her upper body a little. She'd hit her head on that rock—she could see the dark stain of blood on it even in this dim light.

"You should have stayed where you were," she muttered. This far off any recognizable trail, it was going to be even harder for anybody to find her. Panic started to settle in and she fought it off with grim determination.

So she was lost. She'd been through worse—*much* worse. There was no way she could make it up that hill just yet. It was too dark to see well, and with one more accident, she may not be able to make it up that hill at all.

"So I'm stuck here for the night," Kennedy said. "I can handle this."

Hysteria threatened to bubble up and overwhelm her, but she ignored it. "It's your fault you're stuck here—you can handle this."

She undid the pack from her hip and located the small flashlight in it by touch. Kennedy also pulled out the small bottle of Tylenol and popped a couple. Fortunately, her trip down the hill hadn't knocked her water bottle loose and she still had two small nutrition shakes in the pack. The chilly night air was going to be the worst part—well, that and the odd noises that always sounded at night.

She had to move though. There were rocks gouging into her from all over and Kennedy felt too battered already. No way was she sitting on a bed of rocks all night. Scanning the area around her with the flashlight, she decided on the towering pine about ten feet to her right. It would move her that much closer to the hill in the morning and there didn't look to be as many rocks that way.

At first, she tried to stand, but the pain in her head was making her sick and she couldn't bear to put weight on her right ankle. *How undignified...*she sighed morosely as she basically dragged herself the ten feet. Once over there, she used her hand to clear a small area free of pinecones and pine needles and then placed her back against the tree trunk.

She had worn a denim button down earlier and, when she'd gotten hot, tied it around her waist. Now, as she untied the knot and worked it free, Kennedy said a silent prayer of thanks. It wasn't a blanket, but it was something over her bare arms.

Closing her eyes, she leaned her head back against the tree, calling herself ten different kinds of idiot.

"Serve you right if one of those damn cats did show up right about now," she muttered.

Seconds later, her blood turned to ice in her veins as she heard a peculiar, high-pitched scream.

It sounded again seconds later, and it sounded *closer. Should have kept my mouth shut...*

That wasn't a scream.

It was a cougar.

Duncan froze in his tracks as he heard one of the twins screaming into the night.

He threw back his head and screamed back, issuing a summons. Of course, the twins were notoriously arrogant and they didn't like to answer to anybody. Not even the leader of the Pride.

"Damned kids," he swore hotly as he swiftly stripped out of his clothes.

Zane eyed him grimly. "She's not too far."

"They are closer than we are." He couldn't hear her, which meant she wasn't trying to run, thank God. But he smelled one thing that really bothered him.

Blood...

He just hoped the twins had enough control to recognize the difference between an injured mortal woman and acceptable prey. He stood naked in the moonlight for mere seconds as the Change started. He bit back the scream of agony as his bones broke and realigned, going through the Change in utter silence. The second he could breath again, he took off running through the woods.

In this form, his sense of smell was sharper and he smelled not just the blood, but the sharp spicy tang of her fear. It spiked and he knew she had seen the cougars.

He screamed into the night once more as he crested a sharp slope. Staring down it, he saw the twins.

They were circling around a massive pine tree, totally preoccupied with what they saw under it.

Powerful muscles bunched and he jumped, taking the downward slope with swift powerful leaps that landed him in between the twins. He faced the one closest to him, glaring at Deacon with fury.

You were called.

The cougar cocked his head, studying his leader. *We smelled her—she smells good...*

Duncan caught an undertone that had him seeing red. They weren't talking food. Another hunger.

Yes, she did smell good but he wasn't a cub in rut. And he wouldn't allow anybody in his Pride to scare a woman. *Get back. You will return home and pray that I calm down before I talk with you again.*

*Come on, Duncan. She smells so sweet...*That was Douglas and Duncan whirled on him. The cougar was staring at Kennedy and Duncan could have wrung the fool boy's neck as he sensed the power rising in Douglas.

If you Change, I will beat you bloody.

That got a reaction. Both of the twins turned their heads and studied Duncan with wary eyes. Duncan bared his teeth at them, snarling once more in warning. *You will leave—now.*

Their big feline bodies slumped, heads and tails hung low, as they turned and silently padded away.

Duncan didn't bother to watch them leave as he turned and stared at Kennedy.

He was prepared for her terror, braced for the screams he was certain would start at any second. He was even ready for her to run, if she wasn't hurt too badly. He'd have to act then, guiding her away from the twins and toward Zane.

What he wasn't prepared for was the amazement he saw in her eyes.

She stared at him with sheer incredulity. Her lips trembled and her eyes gleamed bright. "Sweet heaven...I was *right...*"

Duncan moved a little closer, trying to see where she was wounded. The smell of blood was old, but he couldn't see any injury. There was no denying it was her blood though. One thing he could see—her right ankle was swollen, more than twice the size it should be. He cast a look up the hill and he could see the path of disturbed earth—she'd tripped, fallen...maybe she hit her head.

He growled a little in his throat, disgusted. So she wasn't going to be able to *walk* out of here and likely had a head injury. Not a serious one, he guessed. If there were any kind of internal bleeding, he would smell that. And she looked a little too aware, her eyes too clear, for the head injury to be serious.

Duncan *hoped.*

From the corner of his eye, he saw her reaching out toward him and he sidestepped, growling a little at her.

You have no sense, he thought darkly, wishing he were in human form so he could yell at her. Out hiking...*alone*...didn't tell a damn soul where she was going to be, and she was trying to pet him. A real cougar would probably take her hand off.

Well, no. A real cougar wouldn't have come this close to her, unless it was to make a meal out of her. Cougars didn't hunt humans, but she was alone and injured—that was enough to taunt any predator that was hungry enough.

Turning away, he started to pace wide circles around the tree, trying not to look at her too closely. As he heard her pushing to her feet, Duncan turned towards her with a soft growl.

Of course, she seemed oblivious. Ether she didn't realize he presented a threat, or that damned head wound was affecting her judgment. Well, he was still assuming she had a head wound.

As she started toward him, he decided it was definitely the latter. Her bad ankle hit the ground and she went white, slamming out a hand to brace her weight against the trunk of the tree. She weaved for a second and he waited for her to sit back down.

Didn't happen though. He heard it as her breathing sped up, as her heart started to race. Just as her eyes started to roll back into her head, Duncan pounced. She collapsed and he caught her weight with his body just before she would have hit the ground.

He heard the soft whisper of air behind him and cocked his head around, staring at Zane darkly.

"Having fun?" Zane asked politely, a smile tugging at the corner of his lips.

Damn it, will you get over here and help me? Duncan thought sourly.

Over the next five minutes, Zane examined Kennedy while Duncan watched. He'd shifted back to human form and tugged on the jeans Zane had tossed at him. The rest of his clothes were folded neatly on the forest floor but Duncan wasn't too interested in them right now.

"Is she going to be okay?"

Zane lifted one shoulder in a shrug as he finished wrapping Kennedy's ankle. "She didn't break anything, but the cut on her head is pretty nasty. She's got a concussion, but I don't know how bad. I wonder how long she was conscious."

Both of them glanced to the south as they heard the others approaching. Nick and Maria stepped out of the trees, each one nodding politely towards Duncan before moving to kneel beside Zane. Zane moved aside, letting Maria take his place.

She was a volunteer member of the local search and rescue team, just like Nick—but her expertise was medical. She was also a paramedic for Pride's lone fire department and the only female member of a fire department in the county.

She glanced at Kennedy's ankle first and glanced at Zane with a faint smile. "You'd make an excellent nurse." Maria was quiet while she probed the head wound, her dark brown eyes unreadable. Finally, she looked up with a sigh. "We need to get her into town. I don't think she cracked her skull, but..."

Her voice trailed away as Kennedy moaned. Duncan moved closer and Nick automatically shifted out of the way as Duncan crouched by Kennedy's other side, across from Maria. The thick fan of her lashes lifted and he found himself staring into bleary eyes.

Her voice was thick and hoarse as she whispered, "I knew you were real." Then she sighed and her lashes lowered once more.

Maria muttered, "What is she talking about?"

Duncan met Zane's eyes. He had a sinking suspicion that he knew what Kennedy was talking about, and judging by the grim look in Zane's eyes, the other man knew, too.

Nobody but the men who were there that night knew what happened fifteen years ago. Well, them...and Kennedy.

The question, though, was just how much did she remember?

Chapter Three

For a minute, when she opened her eyes, Kennedy panicked. Her body ached all over, there were bright white lights shining down in her eyes, and she smelled the astringent scent of cleaners.

In a damned hospital—again.

Before panic could settle in, though, she remembered.

Shit.

Tripping over an exposed root and then lurching to the side. Before she could regain her balance, though, she'd started to fall. Fallen *hard*, if her battered body was any sign. And her head...she groaned a little, reaching up and touching her fingers to the back of her head.

Vaguely, she remembered what happened after. One of *them*...she hissed out a breath. She'd seen one of those cats, a huge beast that looked just like an overgrown cougar. No. More than one. The bigger one had shown up right behind the smaller two. He'd growled at them. For a second, the smaller ones hadn't paid him much attention, but then they'd run away.

She remembered that...then things got blurry. She'd been so excited and tried to stand up—then darkness.

Another vague memory—a man. Shirtless, crouching over her in the moonlight, and staring at her with unreadable golden eyes. Duncan Pride.

After that, just more darkness. Vague memories of a guy in a white coat shining one of those annoying little lights in her eyes, people shaking her gently until she woke up, more lights, questions, more questions.

"So you're awake."

She glanced over as the curtain surrounding her was pushed back and found herself staring into a friendly, cheerful face. "How do you feel?"

Kennedy licked her lips, shaking her head. "My head hurts," she whispered softly.

"I'd imagine so—you've got a big goose egg back there and a moderate concussion," the woman said as she moved a little closer. Her hair was pulled away from her face in a simple ponytail and she had a brightly colored stethoscope around her neck. Her nametag read, *Kari, RN.*

"I'm in the ER?"

"Yes. Let's check your temperature. I can get you something for your headache after I get your vitals."

Headache...hell, that didn't *describe* the pain shooting through her head.

Moments later, Kennedy was alone and she leaned back, closing her eyes as she tried to bring the hazy memories of the past night into focus.

*You could have broke your leg...*The throbbing pain in her ankle reminded her just how lucky she had been. *Or your neck.*

And she didn't care—Kennedy didn't give a damn, because she had *seen* them.

She had no proof and if she tried to tell anybody, not a single person would believe her. But it didn't matter. She'd gone looking for them just to prove to herself she *had* seen them— that something *had* saved her from her stepfather fifteen years ago.

It was amazing, how good vindication felt.

"You look like hell."

Her eyes flew open, her heart skipping a beat at the low, rough voice. Sheriff Duncan Pride stood in the doorway, staring at her with a scowl. Another memory swam up, the image superimposing itself over the man standing in front of her.

Oh, he was still scowling—but he wasn't wearing a shirt and he was crouched over her while she lay on the forest floor.

And disturbingly—the echo of the words she'd whispered to him, *I knew you were real...*

Shaking her head, Kennedy made herself focus on Duncan as he stepped inside the cubicle and pulled the curtain closed behind him. She forced a smile at him and said, "I don't feel much better than that."

"You know your dad would have a fit if he could see you right now," Duncan said shortly. "Cole would probably try to turn you over his knee."

With a faint smile, Kennedy shook her head. "He preferred the more silent approach. He just wouldn't talk to me for a day or two. Lisa, though..."

Duncan snorted in disgust. "Oh, believe me. If Cole and Lisa Franklin had been the ones to find you laying at the bottom of a hill in the middle of a State Park *way* off the trails, they would have been arguing to see who could get to you first." He flipped the sheet up and studied her ankle. "Seriously sprained ankle, moderate concussion. What if you'd broken your neck? What if we hadn't gone looking for you? You're lucky to even be alive, Miz Franklin. "

Rolling her eyes, Kennedy shifted in the bed and fiddled with the control until the bed had her sitting a little more upright. "I'm aware of that, Sheriff. I assume you were there when I was found."

"Yes. One of the park rangers found your truck on the final drive through before she would have left the park. You ruined her night, by the way. We had to call in the search and rescue team—any reason you wandered so far off the trails?" He narrowed his eyes at her and the odd golden color seemed to reflect light back at her.

Kennedy tried to give him a charming smile, but she suspected it fell flat. Shrugging, she said, "I was just trying to find some pretty places to snap pictures." *Pictures...oh, shit.* Squeezing her eyes closed, she whispered, "My camera?"

Duncan arched a brow. "I ought to tell you it's smashed beyond repair."

She breathed out a shaky sigh of relief. "But it's not, right?"

He shook his head. "Zane Matthews found it on the hill as we were moving you out. I didn't mess with it, but it's probably fine." As he crossed his arms over his wide chest, the badge on his belt glinted at her. Another memory slammed into her brain. The last two times she'd seen him, that badge had been worn on his belt.

But he hadn't been wearing it last night...had he?

Just a pair of jeans—she could even remember how those jeans had looked on him, slung low on his hips, a thin ribbon of black hair running down his flat belly, curling around his navel before disappearing under the waist of those jeans.

Just jeans...why was he there wearing just jeans... Then she shook her head. She'd probably dreamed that part. There was a soft little whisper, one she wished vainly she could shut up. *How do you know you didn't dream all of it?*

Clenching her jaw, she forcibly shut that nagging voice up.

"So why were you wandering around?" he asked again.

Kennedy shrugged, fiddling with the nubby weave of the blanket thrown across her legs. "I told you—I wanted to take some pictures."

"Three miles from the nearest trail. Hell, you were almost off state property and on mine."

"Uh..." Three miles. She had known she was lost, but hadn't realized she'd gotten that far off the trail. She dragged her tongue across her lips as she glanced back up to meet his eyes. "I guess I don't have a very good sense of direction."

He laughed, the sound short and harsh, echoing through the brightly lit emergency room. "If that's all it is, I'll say you're sure as hell right. Do us all a favor and carry a compass—and for the love of God, take a guide."

Narrowing her eyes, she crossed her arms over chest and glared at him. "I don't need a damned babysitter."

But even as she said the words, she winced. Before he could open his mouth to comment, she said, "Okay, maybe leaving without a guide was thoughtless. I just wanted to go look around."

Duncan turned away, sighing. He shoved a hand through his hair as he started to pace back and forth across the narrow cubicle. "Next time you feel the need to get close with nature, can you take a guide? It's not smart for *anybody* to go out on a hike alone."

"I'll...I'll be more careful," she said, looking back down at her hands. But she sure as hell couldn't promise she wouldn't go out alone. Not now.

She was even more determined to find out something about these cats.

His piercing gaze felt like it was burning into her skin. Shifting on the bed, she grabbed the control and lowered the bed back down so that she was laying flat once more. Rolling onto her side, she said, "I'm tired."

He didn't say anything else, and for the longest time, it was silent. After a few minutes, she opened her eyes just a little. He was gone—hadn't made a damned sound either.

A week later, Duncan found her at the library. She was seated at one of the old microfiche machines—the current librarian, Carly Banks, had finally gotten the money to update the old system, but there were years and year's worth of articles that had to be added. It wouldn't be complete any time soon.

He started to head her way, but a sketched image on the screen caught his eye. *Shit...*

Over the past two hundred years, the Pride had managed to stay mostly out of sight from others. But every once in a while... Fifty years ago, there had been a sighting of one of the Pride's cougars.

It had been a youth, and like a lot of the males, he'd been careless. The man who had seen him had been the town sheriff—no question about whether or not the story had any credibility. For months, the men in the small city of Pride, Michigan had hunted for the mysterious giant cat.

There hadn't been another sighting since and Duncan knew there wasn't any reliable information. His father had gone through all of the information gathered, but still...now he was beyond uneasy.

Kennedy *knew* about them.

Duncan left without getting the books Carly had on loan from another library. They had a serious problem on their hands and until it was resolved, he wasn't going to have time to read anything more than official business.

Hours later, he sat on the floor in his livingroom, staring into the crackling fire and brooding.

Behind him, Zane and the others spoke quietly. There were three more members of the Pride—Glenna McGuire, Maria Suarez, and Samuel Pride, Duncan's first cousin. The four of them had shown up at Duncan's front porch without him even having to place a call. Duncan was the alpha but these four people were irreplaceable.

They shared a link with the Pride's leader—a psychic alert of sorts. Duncan had known something was wrong, even before Glenna had made the phone call when she saw Kennedy's truck. Zane had had the same feeling and was already on his way to Duncan's.

So it wasn't really a surprise when the four of them showed up.

Not a surprise, but Duncan wished they'd leave him the hell alone as he tried to figure out what to do about this.

"We can call the Council—they have methods of dealing with this sort of thing."

He heard Glenna's comment and bit back a curse. Yeah, he knew the Council's methods. He may have *understood* them, but he sure as hell didn't like them. Kennedy didn't need some vamp from the Council coming out here and blanking her mind.

Even the thought of it had rage sparking through him.

While the others voiced approval of the idea, Duncan stood up. Slowly, he turned and stared at his people. "No."

Zane just closed his eyes, his head falling back on the edge of the couch. Glenna's eyes widened a little while Sam said, "I don't see that we have any other choice."

Duncan simply stared at his cousin.

Maria wisely kept her mouth shut.

Duncan moved across the room, pushing the curtain away from the window as he stared out into the night. Sam rarely understood the concept of thinking before he spoke, but Duncan doubted it would have done any good. Even if Sam *did* think before he spoke, he'd probably still say whatever it was circling through his damned head.

"If you aren't going to call the Council, what are you going to do?" Sam asked flatly. His tone demanded an answer, but Duncan wasn't in any mood to give him one.

He just knew he wasn't going to tolerate a Hunter coming into *his* land, and doing anything to his...

Duncan closed his eyes as the thought completed in his head. *Shit.*

Now this was bad.

Yeah, so what if he'd had a few dreams about her ever since seeing her again, leaning over the counter in her bookstore, twirling a shiny black curl around her finger...a few dreams. Like almost every night.

He refused to think about the blistering rage that had ripped through him when he realized the twins had found Kennedy before he had.

"Damn it, Duncan. Would you stop standing there and brooding? We need a damned answer," Sam growled.

Duncan spun around, his hands curling into loose fists at his side as he glared at his cousin. "I'll handle it." Striding past Sam and the others, he headed for the door.

Zane caught up with him just as Duncan grabbed the door. Duncan whirled around, snarling.

Zane backed away two steps, lifting his hands in front of him. "Calm down, Duncan. You want to handle this, you go ahead and do it." His eyes were calm and Duncan suspected Zane knew exactly why Duncan wasn't calling the damned Council.

"I just want you to think through...whatever it is you're going to do. Okay?"

With a terse nod, Duncan turned around and stalked outside.

Think it through...hell, thinking it through wasn't going to help. He could think it through fifty times and it would still be a bad idea.

But he was going to do it anyway.

Chapter Four

She woke to total silence, but Kennedy knew she wasn't alone. Her heart slammed into her throat as she lay on her side, staring into the darkness of her room, straining to see something beyond the blackness.

Nothing—just shadows upon shadows.

But there was somebody else in the room.

Fear choked her for a minute and she tucked herself into a tight ball, praying she'd just go to sleep and realize this was just a dream.

She heard a soft whisper of sound, a sigh. Coming from near the door. She swallowed and nearly choked on the knot in her throat as a deep rumbling voice said quietly, "Don't be so afraid. I'm not here to hurt you."

Unable to pretend it was just her imagination any more, Kennedy sat up and turned to stare in the direction of the door. It was so damned dark in there—she could barely make out the dark shape standing in the shadows.

His eyes, though...she could see his eyes, flashing at her in the dark. Golden, glowing, eerie as hell—

"The cats you've been looking for—why?"

Kennedy blinked. She hadn't said a damn thing to *anybody*. How in the hell did he know?

"I...ah—I'm not looking for any cats," Kennedy said and cursed as she heard how wobbly her voice was, how weak and pathetic she sounded.

"Don't give me that. I saw you in the forest—I know you've been looking for them. Why?"

Ooookay... Kennedy licked her lips as she shifted on the bed. "Do you mind turning on the light?"

"Yes."

Narrowing her eyes, she demanded, "Okay, how about telling me who in the hell you are and how you got in here?"

"I picked the lock." She thought for a second she heard the slightest bit of humor in that deep, grumbly voice. The sound of it made shivers run up and down her spine, but she didn't really feel afraid. Not any more.

"And...?"

"And what?"

"Who in the hell are you?" she snapped, exasperated. She sure as hell couldn't place that gruff voice and it was too damned dark for her to see—although his eyes, they continued to gleam at her.

Cat's eyes...

"If I wanted to tell you who I was, I would have made an appointment, sweetheart."

He moved forward, but kept to the shadows, avoiding the faint light that shone in through the window as he neared the bed. "Now...why don't you tell me what I want to know?"

She caught her lower lip between her teeth as she tried to figure out if there was even any point to playing dumb. It hadn't worked so far. Blowing out a sigh, she pushed a hand through her hair. It tangled in the curls and she absently started to finger comb the knot away. "I saw them before. I...I just wanted to know if I really saw them. Wanted to know more about them."

"What exactly do you want to know about them, Kennedy?"

The sound of her name on his lips made her quiver. An odd heat moved through her and she shifted on the bed, drawing her knees to her chest as the heat spread and turned into an ache. "Just...just more. They're big for cougars—and I didn't think cougars liked people."

"They don't."

Kennedy scowled at him. "I was attacked fifteen years ago—these cougars saved me. They sure as hell didn't mistake me for a cub."

A low chuckle came out of the dark. Kennedy narrowed her eyes, trying to see him better.

"No, they didn't think you were a cub."

He moved a little closer and Kennedy froze as he bent over the bed. Close...so close she could feel his body heat, smell the warm earthy scent of his skin. Her heart lodged in her throat and she kicked free from the blankets, rolling away from him and out of the bed. Standing by the window, she glared at him. "I answered your question—now why don't you get the hell out?"

"You're awful brave for a woman alone in a house with a man she doesn't know."

The fear choking her threatened to bubble out in hysterical screams, but she desperately swallowed them down. *Damn it, I will not freak out.* Tossing her hair back, she said coolly, "If you were going to hurt me, wouldn't you have done it already?"

"Maybe...or maybe I wanted to hear what you had to say first. Besides, seeing you standing in the moonlight wearing nothing but a t-shirt..." His voice trailed off into a soft laugh. "You look nice in the moonlight—I imagine you'd look even better if you weren't wearing that t-shirt."

Kennedy swallowed, folding her arms protectively around her middle. Maybe she should scream. A dry cynical voice in her head whispered, *Maybe you should have done that like five minutes ago...*

"If it will make you feel better, go ahead and scream. Nobody will hear you. And I meant what I said—I'm not going to hurt you."

"Then what are you doing here?" she demanded.

"You need to forget you saw those cats, Kennedy. They don't concern you."

Slowly, she shook her head. "I can't. I've tried to forget about them for the past fifteen years. I have to know."

"What do you have to know?"

Tears clogged her throat, burned her eyes but she finally forced the words out. "Why they saved me."

⁂

For a minute, he thought his heart was going to break.

Duncan waited until she looked away and then he moved, sliding up until he stood right next to her. He spun her around and wrapped his arms around her waist, covering her hands with his. Kennedy stiffened at his touch and he rubbed his thumb against the back of her hand.

"Hush...I won't hurt you..."

Shapeshifters could use fear—the more powerful ones could exude an aura of it that could freeze people in their tracks. There was a flipside to that power though. They could also learn to use it to calm fear. That was what he did now, reaching out and trying to calm the fear that had wrapped itself around Kennedy.

"They are not normal cougars, Kennedy...they aren't even cougars at all. They resemble them, especially from a distance, but they aren't cougars. And they saved you because it's what they do. Make no mistake...they are predators, but they prey on those who'd prey on others."

Slowly, he reached up, touching one hand to her disheveled hair, smoothing it back from her face. "There's nothing more I can tell you about them. But you need to leave them be. There are some things in life that just can't be explained. This is one of them."

He could see the pale oval of her face, reflected in the mirror. He kept his head ducked low to keep her from being able to see any of his features—it was for the best, he knew.

But part of him wanted...no...part of him *needed* to see her in the light, to let her see him.

Duncan hadn't ever wanted a mate. His mother had died in childbirth and his father had spent the rest of his life missing her. Zane—he'd lost his mate young as well. Giving your heart seemed to do little more than open you to pain.

"If it can't be explained, then how come you know so much about them?" Kennedy asked huskily.

Sliding his hands up her arms, he laid them in the curve between her neck and shoulder. He could feel the pounding of her pulse against his fingertips. Duncan lowered his head and murmured in her ear, "Maybe I'm another one of those things that can't be explained."

He flexed his hands against the satin of her skin, reveling in the soft, smooth warmth. Then he stepped back, reaching out to trail one hand down her hair. It was every bit as soft as her skin and smelled like honeysuckle. "Good-bye, Kennedy."

Hours later, Kennedy lay in bed, staring out her window as the sun crept over the horizon. She hadn't gone back to sleep.

Everything felt disconnected, distorted.

Fifteen years. She'd waited fifteen years and had gotten so close. Part of her whispered, *Nothing has changed...whoever he was, he can't stop you.*

But the larger, more logical part of her brain said otherwise. There had been an implacability to his words that warned her—she had to let this go.

She sighed, turned her face into her pillow. "You need to just go back to Detroit."

And do what?

Kennedy couldn't go back to social work.

There had been a crack in her heart caused by what she'd lived through before she went to the Franklins. The love she'd known there had healed that crack, but it had been ripped violently back open when she had she had gone to Marisa Armstrong's house to find out why she had missed her appointment and found the teenage girl swinging from a noose made of sheets.

She'd been dead for more than a day—and probably would have continued to hang there for several days, unnoticed, if Kennedy hadn't gone looking for her. Even though she had been returned to her mother's care, Marisa might as well have lived all alone for all the attention she received.

Tears leaked out from under her closed lids and she took a deep, shuddering breath. "What am I going to do?"

Coming back here had seemed so right at the time. Even beyond trying to find out more about the cougars...*They aren't cougars.* That deep rumble of a voice echoed in her head. Her lids drooped shut as she tried to block the memory of his voice out.

Even if she hadn't wanted to know more about the cats, coming back here, taking over the bookstore her adopted parents had given her, this had all seemed like the right choice.

She'd been worried at first—worried everybody would look at her and remember.

That seeing her old town would stir up memories of what had happened to her here, but it hadn't.

She had just felt like she was home, and the feeling only intensified the longer she was here. Now after nearly two months, Kennedy felt like she was *home*. She hadn't felt like this since she had lived here with the Franklins.

Could she leave?

She just didn't know. She didn't want to.

The longer she was here, the more obsessed she had become with learning about the cats. Could she stay here and ignore that burning need?

Hours passed as she lay there. Did she stay—did she go? Who had that guy been? How had he known about the cats? What did she do now?

All those questions circled endlessly through her mind and she had no more an answer by the time nine o'clock came and went then she had six hours earlier.

The phone rang and she ignored it, reaching down and pulling the heavy down quilt over her head. After five rings, the answering machine came on and she heard Leslie's concerned voice. Dismally, she told herself she should answer. Leslie was probably worried about her.

But she just let the woman rattle on the machine and when the machine cut her off, Kennedy rolled over onto her other side and closed her eyes.

Maybe things would make more sense if she got some sleep.

Duncan muttered to himself as he turned down the long drive that led to Kennedy's house. "This is a *bad* idea."

He'd been uneasy, restless, frustrated, ever since leaving here hours earlier. That was why he had gone by *A Page Apart*. He'd wanted to see Kennedy.

But she hadn't been there and Leslie had looked at him with beseeching eyes. "It's just not like her to not call—she's run late before, but she always called."

Duncan had replied, "She does own the place. Maybe she just wanted to sleep in a little. Kennedy knew you were going to be here, right?"

Leslie just gave him that look and Duncan had sighed, already giving in.

"I called her house, Duncan. Nobody answered."

Nothing was wrong. He told himself that, insisted she was just sleeping, even as he parked in front of the old farmhouse. His eyes were gritty from lack of sleep. He hadn't slept at all last night and work today was going to be a trial.

He also knew if he didn't check on Kennedy, the worry would eat at him all day and he'd be useless as hell.

The first knock on the door went unanswered, but he could hear her faintly through the walls. Resting a hand on the glass window next to the door, he closed his eyes and concentrated.

Sleeping...just like he'd thought. The slow, steady sound of her breath changed as he knocked a second time and he heard the increase in her heart rate as she woke up.

He let his hand fall away from the window as he waited for her to answer the door. It took a minute, but he could hear the slow tread of her footsteps as she climbed from bed and moved towards the front of the house.

She opened the door and Duncan started to smile, only to feel it fall from his face as a leaden weight settled in the pit of his belly. Her eyes were red and swollen, and her face was pale.

Frowning, he studied her wan face for a moment before he said, "You look even worse than you did last week."

Kennedy just blinked at him, leaning against the doorjamb as she stared at him. She kept her ankle up off the floor and he glanced at it, noting that it was still swollen, still bruised. "I was in the store. Leslie said you hadn't shown up, didn't call. She was a little worried."

Kennedy pushed her hair back from her face. "I'm fine. I'll call her here in a few minutes."

"Are you okay?" he asked softly.

Her pretty gray eyes stared sightlessly over his shoulder as she shrugged. "Tired. Just tired."

"You sure? Everything okay in there?"

She smiled faintly. "Oh, everything is just peachy, Sheriff. You have a good day."

And just like that, she closed the door, dismissing him.

※✦◈✦◈✦※

Kennedy called Leslie, insisting she'd just had a bad night and overslept. No, she didn't hear the phone ring, and she was sorry she had worried anybody. Yes, yes, she'd be fine, just needed a little more rest. Would things be okay at the store?

After convincing Leslie she was fine, she hung up the phone and made her way slowly back to bed. Her right ankle was still sore and she had to brace her weight against the wall. By the time she got to bed, it was throbbing and she ended up bypassing the bed for the bathroom so she could wash down one of the pain pills she'd been prescribed before leaving the ER.

Wearily, she went back to bed and pulled the covers over her face.

She tumbled into sleep with the promise she'd start trying to think again after she'd rested.

Chapter Five

Between her sleepless night and the pain pill, Kennedy slept the day away. She opened her eyes to total darkness and experienced a weird dejà vu as she sat up. The events of the night before had infiltrated even her dreams and she had tossed and turned while that deep, sexy voice whispered to her.

Now, as she sat on the edge of the bed, she realized that she wasn't leaving.

And she also wasn't letting some nameless, faceless man make her quit.

Shoving her tangled hair away from her face, she gripped the nightstand and slowly stood up, gingerly putting weight on her ankle. Still sore—but she figured she could make it through a shower and then she'd put the brace on.

The hot spray of water helped wash the rest of the cobwebs from her mind and when she climbed out of the stall, she felt a lot clearer than she had felt since her mystery visit. After slicking her skin with lotion, she grabbed the ankle brace she kept on the back of the toilet and put it on.

The support helped a lot and as she walked out of the bathroom, the pain was almost non-existent.

"Turn off the light."

At the sound of that deep, gruff voice, Kennedy froze. Her eyes scanned the room and she found his shadow, standing by the window. He'd pulled the curtains and lowered the blinds—

the only light came from the bathroom. But she stood *right* there. She sure as hell wasn't ready to enter another conversation with him under the cloak of darkness.

"No. What are you doing here? Didn't we finish this conversation yesterday...or wait, that was this morning, wasn't it?" she said, not caring that her voice sounded a little bitchy.

She could feel him staring at her and her skin burned. Blood rushed to her cheeks and she folded her arms over her chest. The towel she had tucked around her suddenly felt far too thin, far too insubstantial.

"I was right..." he murmured. "You look even better without the t-shirt."

Kennedy could feel the heat in his voice and it made her shiver, made her belly clenched with need. Sexual desire was something she'd spent most of her life shying away from. She wouldn't deny it—what her stepfather had done to her had damaged something inside and she just didn't know how to fix it. But more than that, she had never really felt compelled to fix it. The men in her past who had been attracted to her had never made her feel anything.

But with this man...she was acutely aware of every inch of exposed skin, of the way the cool air felt on her flesh, of the rough timbre of his voice. His voice seemed a little deeper tonight, a little more raspy. Dragging her tongue over her lips, she clutched the towel a little tighter to her chest. "I'd like to put some clothes on," she said, hoping her voice didn't sound as shaky as she felt.

"Go ahead," he offered softly. "I'll even turn my back."

"Leave."

He chuckled. "You have a nice big walk in closet over there. Walk in."

Narrowing her eyes, Kennedy muttered, "I really don't like you."

She heard him breathe in softly, then blow his breath back out. "I almost wish that was true...get dressed, Kennedy. I'm trying to be nice right now. It probably won't last."

Kennedy glared in his direction before stalking across the room, well, half stalking. It was hard to do it effectively when her ankle was still half lame. She flicked on the light before closing the door tightly behind her.

No damn lock on the door. Grabbing a pair of jeans from the shelf in front of her, Kennedy dragged them on over her still damp body.

No underwear. All of that was in the dresser out in the bedroom. Worse...no bra. Kennedy hissed out a breath and grabbed the first thing that came to hand, a white button down that was three sizes too big. Her fingers raced over the buttons, securing them from the neck all the way down before she rolled the long sleeves up until she could push them over her elbows.

When she opened the door, the first thing she saw was the bathroom light. Off.

"Turn that light off."

Kennedy crossed her arms over her chest. "No."

He laughed and asked, "Are you going to stand there in the door way all night?"

"No," she replied, stripping the towel from her hair and combing her fingers through the damp strands. "Just until you leave."

"You're stubborn, aren't you?"

"Why don't you tell me why in the hell you're here now?" she asked tiredly, leaning against the doorjamb and relaxing her right leg so she could take some of the weight off her ankle.

"Why don't you sit down before that ankle starts hurting again?" he asked levelly.

She glared at him but knew if she stayed on her feet too long, her ankle would start to swell, brace or no brace. And if the damned thing started to swell, the pain would come back. Hell, she had taken off three days because of her ankle and the days she had gone to work, she'd spent most of them in the office doing paperwork with her ankle propped up.

She moved over to the large armchair that was in the corner just to her left. It was close to the closet—he wasn't going to come that close to the light. But even before she had managed to get her ankle up on the matching ottoman, the light clicked off behind her.

She froze, lifting her eyes and watching him as he moved to stand at the edge of the chair. Once more, the room was shrouded in darkness and she could see nothing more than the glitter of his eyes. How had he moved that fast...it hadn't even taken him two seconds to cross her room, in utter silence, and turn off that light.

With a weary sigh, she leaned her head back against the pillowed cushion. "Do you just really dislike light or is this all about keeping us from seeing each other?"

He laughed, crouching down beside the chair. His hand came up and touched her cheek, unerringly. "I can see you just fine."

And she had no doubt of that.

His thumb swept across her cheek in a slow motion. "You have the softest skin," he mused. "And you smell so sweet."

At that moment, her mind seemed to just shut down. Her heart skittered in her chest and she sucked air in desperately. She could just barely make out the faint outline of his head as he moved closer. "I...uh..."

But whatever she was going to say simply died as he closed the distance between them and covered her mouth with his. Other than his hand cupping her cheek and his mouth on hers, he didn't touch her. He traced his tongue along the lines of her lips, slowly, gently.

Kennedy shivered, scared, unsure. He kept his movements slow and unhurried, not trying to do anything more than explore the contours of her mouth. Long moments passed as she sat there, frozen. *She* didn't know what to do—her body, though...her body reacted slowly, a warmth starting to burn in the pit of her belly and spreading outward.

Her pulse sped up as he traced his tongue over the seam of her lips. Slowly, she opened her mouth and felt his harsh intake of breath just before he slowly pushed inside. His hand shifted from her cheek to cup over the back of her neck, angling her head back.

She groaned and arched closer to him as he started to kiss her deeper. Kennedy shifted on the chair, turning toward him. Slowly, she ran her hands up his arms, curling her fingers into the ridge of the muscle atop his shoulders.

One big, warm hand curved around her hip as she tried to move closer to him. The heat of his body seemed to burn through the layers of clothing and she strained against him. He groaned and the sound of it rumbled against her chest as he tore his mouth away.

"Damn it, Kennedy," Duncan rasped, lowering his head to rest his brow on her shoulder for a second. He could feel her heart beat, slamming in her chest, against his own. The taste of her buzzed through his system, making his own heart race, heating his blood until he thought it was going to start to boil.

He hadn't lied when he said he could see her just fine—hell, he could see her *too* fine. The white shirt she'd pulled on covered her completely, but he could see the dark circles of her nipples as they pressed against the cotton.

Her nails bit into his shoulders again, a sweet little pain that did nothing to clear the thick cloud that had enveloped his brain. Skimming hands up her arms, he closed his hands around her neck, his thumbs resting in the hollow there. "You're going to drive me out of my mind," he muttered.

He used one hand to brush her hair back and lowered his head, raking his teeth lightly across her neck. She turned her head towards his as he lifted up and her mouth covered his again. He swallowed that soft, pleading moan even as the logical little voice in his head insisted he needed to stop.

This time, when he tried to pull away, Kennedy came with him and he arched up against her as she came down to straddle his lap, one knee on either side of his hips. Now the aching flesh of his cock was pressing against her sex. Even through the tight, sturdy denim that covered him, he could feel her heat.

And worse—he could smell her. The scent of hungry woman filled the air and it taunted the beast lurking so close under the surface. His hands clamped over her hips as she started to rock against him. Her tongue slowly trailed over his lips before pushing inside his mouth. Duncan bit down softly before sucking on her, pulling her in deeper. She pressed against him, her knees tightening around his hips.

His control damned near shattered and he tore his mouth away, lifting his face to the ceiling as he panted for breath. "Kennedy—we have to stop this."

Her lips roamed over the skin of his neck, leaving burning trails of sensation. She made a soft little hum under her breath and when she spoke, her voice was thick, almost drugged sounding. "I like the way you taste."

The air was heavy with the scent of her hungry body and Duncan groaned, squeezing his eyes closed in a desperate attempt to find control again.

It was a losing battle. If she wanted him to stop, he could have. He knew that.

But the gentle, careful kiss he had given her had exploded into a hot, wicked desire that he was certain would burn them both. He reached up, threading his hands through her hair and forcing her to hold still. He knew she couldn't see him. There was just the faintest light that penetrated the covered window and that was the only light in the room. She couldn't see him—but she needed to listen.

"Kennedy—just...*stop* for a second," he demanded as she tried to lean into him once more. He couldn't completely understand how this had gotten so out of control, but he'd be damned if he didn't give her one more warning.

"Listen, you know where this is heading, don't you?" he said.

Her hands roamed restlessly over his shoulders. *Damn it, did she even hear him?* he wondered.

Gritting his teeth, Duncan stood up, keeping her locked against him. He pumped his hips between her thighs, making sure she felt the burning length of him. "You feel this, Kennedy?" He pivoted toward the bed and laid her down, coming down on top of her, preparing himself to move away if he sensed even the slightest bit of fear. She just arched against him, another one of those greedy little moans falling from her lips. He streaked a hand up her side, cupping her naked breast through the thin layer of cotton. Duncan rubbed his thumb over the pebbled flesh before he lowered his head and bit her gently. "Feel that?"

She hissed, her hands cupping up to fist in his hair, clutching him to her. "You know where this is going?" he repeated, moving against the pull of her hands to whisper into her ear. "We keep this up for any longer and it's going to be too late."

Kennedy turned her head, once more finding his mouth with unerring skill. "It's already too late," she whispered. "Please...I want to feel this."

Her hips rocked against him. Slowly, Duncan sat up, bracing one knee on either side of her hips. Reaching for the strip of buttons on her shirt, he opened them slowly, still staring at her face. Her eyes stared blindly up and Duncan wished he could turn the lights on.

He wanted to see her in the golden glow of the sun, in the silvery light of the moon...and more, he wanted *her* to see *him.* As he finished unbuttoning her shirt, he levered his weight off of her and whispered, "Sit up."

She sat up slowly and he stripped the shirt off. "Pretty," he whispered, trailing his fingers over the curve of one breast. He ran one finger down the center of her chest, circling around her navel before slipping his fingertips inside the waistband of her jeans.

Kennedy lay back on her elbows, her eyes closing. The black banner of her hair spilled around her shoulders to curl in ribbons against the comforter. As he freed the button on her jeans, the smooth plain of her belly undulated in a shuddering breath. He kept his eyes on her face as he stripped her jeans away. Running his hands up the outside of her legs, he crouched back between her thighs, staring up at her face.

"Don't be afraid of me," he muttered gruffly as he bent over her, using his hands to push her weight further across the bed so he could lie between her thighs. The ripe scent of her need called to him and he had to taste her.

Slowly, he stroked his tongue over the naked folds of her sex. She cried out, a harsh, startled sound, her hands flying up to fist in his hair. Duncan hadn't ever felt so aware—not of another woman, not of himself. His senses were sharply attuned to her, bracing for just the slightest sign of fear.

But all he could sense was hungry woman. He growled against her as she arched her hips up to his mouth. Using his fingers, he opened the honey-slicked folds of her sex and speared his tongue inside her. At the same time, he pressed his thumb against the firm little bud of her clit.

She sobbed as he changed position, lifting his mouth to suckle on her clit and pushing his two fingers inside her sheath. She was tight and wet, clenching around his fingers in a tight, convulsing grip.

He pushed her into one screaming climax before rising to his knees, his eyes searching out her face. Her skin was coated with a light sheen of sweat, her eyes wide and glassy. He could just barely make out the light flush that stained her skin, spreading upward from the hard-tipped curves of her breasts to her brow.

Damn it—Duncan was certain if he didn't get inside her, completely inside her, he was going to go out of his mind. Lust was a burning hot demon that rode his back and threatened to choke him. His hands shook as he reached up and tore his shirt away. As it drifted to the floor, he stood up and kicked his shoes off, stripping his jeans away.

Naked, he moved to cover her, fisting one hand in her hair and staring down into her face.

"Last chance, Kennedy," he whispered as he pressed against her. His cock nestled between her folds and he tortured himself by dragging his length back and forth.

She arched against him, her hands sliding up over his shoulders, the bite of her nails into his flesh urging him on.

Duncan shifted a little, using his knees to spread her thighs wider before he pressed against her, slowly pushing inside her. As the tight hot silk of her tissues sheathed the first inch of his cock, Duncan groaned, lowering his head to press his brow against hers. "Damn it, Kennedy..."

In that second, her body went stiff and the rapid cadence of her heartbeat became more erratic, her breath skipping. The scent of her body changed just a little as fear began to invade her body.

"Wait..." It was a soft, pitiful little plea and Duncan gritted his teeth, knowing this was going to kill him.

He started to pull away and she sobbed, her hands still clutching at his arms. "Shhh...it's okay," he murmured. "I'm not going to do anything else."

But when he pulled away, she reached for him. Duncan caught her hands, lying down next to her. "It's okay," he whispered gruffly, pressing a kiss to her temple.

"It's *not*," she choked out. She was trembling, shudders wracking her entire body. "Damn it, I won't let him do this..."

"Kennedy, it's okay. I won't—"

She moved against him and Duncan felt her hands pressing into his chest. He fell backward and she moved forward, straddling his thighs. "I won't let *him* stop me," she muttered, her eyes dark, determined.

As her hand closed over his cock, he felt his flesh jerk. "Shit," he rasped, staring down and watching as she held him steady and slowly started to take him inside.

"I want this—you. I haven't wanted anybody...*ever*..." Her voice trailed off and she moaned, the sound hitching in her chest.

Her eyes drifted closed as she worked her hips up and down, taking a little more of his length inside with each downward stroke. Duncan slid his hands up her thighs, cupping her hips in his hands. Everything inside him wanted to grab and throw her to her back, drive his length in deep and hard and fast. He wanted to mark her flesh, cover her with his scent...but instead he lay there.

She rode him slowly, the motions of her hips awkward. Duncan squeezed her flesh gently and slowly eased her into a smooth rhythm. "Bend down," he whispered and as she did, he lifted his head and caught one swollen nipple in his mouth.

As he laved the nipple, she clenched around him. Involuntarily, Duncan arched up, driving his cock deep and hard as his hands clutched at her hips, holding her locked into him.

She cried out, but it wasn't a panicked cry. Duncan moved to the other breast as he circled against her. Kennedy moaned and Duncan laid his head back on the bed, staring up at her as he lifted her weight a little and started to pump his hips upward, driving his length in and then withdrawing before he plunged deep inside her again.

Kennedy's sex tightened around his cock. The scent of her body suddenly spiked, flooding the air. He felt the trembling in her limbs, the tightening of her sex and then her head fell back and she screamed. He stiffened underneath as she climaxed, pumping into her hard and fast as fire streaked down his spine and licked at his sac.

He exploded into her, groaning out her name. Reaching up, he caught a fist of her hair and jerked her down to him. He bit her lower lip but didn't kiss her, instead pushing her hair aside and setting his teeth on the curve of her neck, biting down in the firm resilient flesh.

The taste of her flooded his system and Duncan moaned, letting go of her hair to slide his arms around her waist. She collapsed against his chest, her chest heaving raggedly with every breath.

* * *

Long moments passed as she lay cuddled against his chest, her breathing finally leveling out. Kennedy licked her lips, reveling in the salty taste that clung to her mouth. *Him...*she was tasting him. Tasting his flesh on her lips.

His hand stroked up and down her back, his heart beat slow and steady in her ear. It had been racing like freight train moments ago. *She* had done that.

Kennedy's initiation to sex had been brutal and cruel. It had scarred her, kept her from getting close to any man that tried.

This man, whoever he was, hadn't tried. He just did it.

"Are you okay?" he asked quietly.

Her lips curled into a smile and she whispered, "Oh, yes." She was *more* than okay. She lifted up, staring down at his face. Her eyes had adjusted a little and she could faintly make out the line of his jaw and when he smiled, she could see the white flash of his teeth.

As she moved, his flesh twitched inside her. He was still firm, but no longer so hard it almost bruised her flesh. She clenched around him, moaning a little. She licked her lips, squeezing her eyes tightly closed for a second.

There was something she wanted to ask him...

Finally, the question made sense in her head once again. Her cheeks flushed as she asked, "How did you know what happened to me?" She bit her lip the second she asked it, unsure of how he was going to answer. "How do you know me?"

He shifted, gently moving her off of him, but he didn't leave. Instead he urged her down onto her side, rolling over so that he could spoon up behind her. His hand rested on her hip as he whispered, "I know what happens around here, Kennedy. And I know you—have for years."

She tried to turn around and look towards him, but he tightened his grip on her hip and she pursed her lips in a sulk. "Are you ever going to let me know who you are?"

His soft laugh teased her skin and he murmured, "I think after tonight, I pretty much have to. Just...not yet."

"Then when?"

He arched against her and she felt that dangerous heat start to shimmer through her. He was long and hard again, the steely length burning into her buttocks. "The next time I come over, maybe," he whispered.

"Next time?" she repeated, her mind going dull, need swelling up and dimming everything else.

"Yes. Next time. And there will be a next time, and one after that...and after that..." He pressed his lips to her shoulder. "When I said it was almost too late, Kennedy...I wasn't just talking about sex."

***

He wasn't there when Kennedy woke up. As she stretched, she felt aches in places she'd forgotten she even possessed. Smiling, she closed her eyes as she breathed in deep.

She could still smell him on the smooth cotton of her sheets, on her own skin.

Her sense of smell seemed almost vividly clear and as she licked her lips, she realized she could still taste him on her mouth. She slid her hand down the empty space next to her, but the sheets were cool.

He'd been gone a while.

A slow smile curled her lips as she sat up, drawing her knees to her chest and hugging them. He would come back.

Again and again, he had whispered before he eased her onto her back and slowly pushed back inside her.

Some twenty minutes later, she finally stopped reveling in the memories and climbed from the bed. She started toward the bathroom, but stopped. No...she didn't want to wash his scent away, not yet. Instead, she grabbed the shirt he had stripped away from her last night.

"This just might become my favorite shirt," she said with a smile as she tugged it on and buttoned it up.

She padded from the room, heading for the kitchen. She was starving—after sleeping yesterday away, and last night...well, it had been a lot more energetic than she was used to. If she didn't get something in her belly soon, she just might start chewing on the walls.

Fortunately, she still had eggs and bacon.

She had bacon simmering within minutes and the rich scent of it had her drooling. Unable to wait for it to be done, she popped a piece of bread in the toaster. The minute it popped out, she grabbed it and tore off a big bite, groaning with pleasure.

While she waited on the bacon, she poured herself a glass of juice and started whipping up eggs for an omelet.

Sunday—she glanced towards the clock, but dismissed the idea of trying to get ready for church. Not today. She'd have to shower.

And Kennedy still wasn't ready to wash his scent away.

"You'd better get over that before you go back into work," she mumbled, shaking her head, a little amazed.

But then she pressed her nose against her arm and breathed deep. Even through the clean scent of her cotton shirt, she could smell him. Warm, musky male.

Grinning, she leaned back against the counter and waited for her breakfast to finish cooking.

Chapter Six

Duncan lifted his beer in a salute as Zane mounted the stairs. He took another sip before gesturing to the front door. "More inside."

Zane shook his head. "No, thanks. Not staying too long." He leaned against the railing, studying Duncan with narrowed eyes. "You look like you had a good night."

He couldn't stop the smug grin that spread across his face. He was going back there tonight—and tonight, he'd keep the lights on. As he left her house this morning, the early light of predawn lighting the way as he ran home, he had realized what had happened last night.

Dad had told him how he had bonded with his mate the very first time he'd seen her. If she hadn't died giving birth to Duncan's younger brother twenty-five years ago, she would have grown old with his dad. Maybe his dad would even be alive...he might have retired earlier, and maybe he wouldn't have been the one who faced down that feral.

*No...it could have been me...*Sighing, Duncan ran a hand over his face.

He missed his dad—but Duncan couldn't deny that he was damned glad he hadn't been the one taking the silver bullet in his chest. He would have missed finding Kennedy again.

When it happens, son, you'll know...you'll have your destiny right there in front of you and everything will make sense.

As always, Ryan Pride had been right. Duncan had Kennedy—she was mortal, she was still a little broken inside, but none of that mattered. Everything would be fine.

"You look pretty damn smug."

Duncan looked up and saw the irritation written all over his old friend's face, but he didn't really care. "So what if I do?" he asked with an easy smile.

"Was this how you planned on solving the problem? By taking her as your mate?" Zane said, his voice flat.

Arching a brow, Duncan took another drink from his beer before he set the bottle down. He stood up then, slowly, and crossed the porch to stare into Zane's eyes. "No. It's not how I planned it—but that's obviously how it was meant to be," he told his lieutenant coldly. "And I'm fairly certain I don't have to answer to you on how I choose to live my private life."

Zane glared at him. "Damn it, son, your private life affects the lives of more than three hundred other people. Have you forgotten about the Pride?"

"No. I haven't forgotten the Pride. I'll never forget the Pride. I know who I am and what my responsibilities are. But...she is my mate, the one woman who was made just for me, just as I was made for her. That didn't happen by accident or by any choice I've made. It happened because that's how it was meant to happen." Cocking his head, Duncan murmured, "You know, I expected this from Sam, but the way you acted, I thought you'd understand."

"I had no fucking idea you were going to *mate* with her!" Zane growled. The green striations in his eyes began to glow, widening until the green glow had spread over the hazel. The fury exuding from him stained the air all around him. "She's *mortal.*"

Duncan said quietly, "So was your wife."

Zane stumbled back, the anger that flooded him draining away and leaving the man standing there, looking gray and gaunt.

But Duncan didn't back down. "I will not have my life dictated by the beliefs or desires of others. My father made sure I understood my responsibilities, Zane, to the Pride and to myself."

Turning away, he walked over to the chair and grabbed his beer from the floor. Glancing at Zane, he said quietly, "You are to speak of this with *no one*. I'll tell the Pride—when I am ready." He headed for the door only to freeze as Zane spoke once more.

"And how long will you hide it?" Zane asked sourly.

Narrowing his eyes, Duncan said, "I hide nothing. But when I tell the Pride, I bring my mate with me. Which means I need to explain things to her." He reached to open the door, but before he stepped inside, he paused to cast one last look at Zane. "Remember what I said, Zane. You are not to speak of this."

As the sun started to sink behind the horizon, Kennedy leaned her head back against the rim of the tub. The hot water felt unbelievably good.

Was he going to come tonight?

She didn't know, but if he did, she wanted to be ready. She'd already shaved her legs, washed her hair, done a conditioning rinse. Now she was soaking in oil-scented water. Kennedy had a weakness for bath oils. She loved how her skin felt, loved the scent that clung to her skin.

She glanced at the picture window over the bathtub, seeing complete dark had settled. This bathroom had been a gift from Cole to Lisa on the thirtieth anniversary. The sunken tub was centered right at the sill of the picture window and she could stare out into the lush garden that Lisa had worked so hard on.

A sad little smile curved her lips as she sat up and pulled the drain. As the water emptied out, she stepped from the tub and grabbed the robe she'd hung on the hook.

Lisa had loved her bathroom, said it made her feel like a queen. Cole had laughingly told her she *was* a queen. It had been one of the very few trips that Kennedy had come here for a visit, instead of them visiting her in Detroit.

She left the bathroom and padded out of the huge bedroom. She couldn't sleep in there—in her mind, that room belonged to her parents, the only parents she'd ever really known. As she walked down the hall to her room, she tugged the towel from her hair.

After smoothing some gel through the heavy curls, she shrugged out of her robe and pulled on the pajamas she had left laying on her bed. They were silvery gray, the top a camisole with skinny straps, the pants with a loose drawstring. She tied the waist so that they hung a little lower on her hips and walked back into the bathroom to stare at her reflection.

Well, it wasn't Hollywood glamorous, but Kennedy didn't even own a slinky negligee so this would have to work. Besides, she'd feel incredibly stupid walking around the house in a teddy.

Tension had her muscles knotted and tight and she headed for the kitchen. There was a bottle of wine in the fridge and she uncorked it, pouring a full glass. She left it on the counter—if he didn't show up, she might need more just so she could relax enough to sleep.

Hearing a car coming toward the house, she smiled a little. A thrill of anticipation ran through her and she left the kitchen.

Or she could always use the wine and drink herself into oblivion, she mused a moment later as she moved to stare out the living room window.

It was her mother.

In the past two months, she had seen Kelly Masters only three times.

And each time, Kelly had been ugly, nasty, and full of bitterness. *Where is he...you chased him off...where is my husband...*

In her gut, Kennedy knew that Kelly knew the truth. Knew that Jack was dead. And she also knew Kelly was aware of what Jack had done to his stepdaughter.

She'd denied it in the hospital, insisted Kennedy was lying even when the doctors told her there was indefinable proof that Kennedy been raped.

You little slut—I knew you were chasing after him.

Those voices still rang in her head and as she stared at her mother, Kennedy almost just slammed the door.

Instead, she tossed her hair back from her face and said coolly, "Hello, Kelly."

This woman may have given birth to her, but the woman Kennedy considered her mom was buried.

Kelly laughed and it was an ugly, bitter sound. Years of smoking and drinking had made the woman's throat hoarse and raspy. "Now that doesn't sound like a girl happy to see her mama."

A tight smile curled Kennedy's mouth briefly as she responded, "My mama is dead. She died in a car wreck with her husband a few months ago. You...you're nothing to me."

Kelly sneered at Kennedy. "You little bitch—I gave you life!"

"And you also left me alone with a monster. You know what he did to me—hell, you might have known he was going to do it before it happened. And you didn't care. Hell, you *defended* him. You blamed me!" Kennedy snarled. The fury surging through her veins was a long time coming, but it felt good. It felt...clean.

"You asked for it—damn it, I saw how you were always walking around the house, wearing nothing but clothes like...like that," Kelly hissed, gesturing towards the pajamas Kennedy had put on.

Glancing down, Kennedy just shrugged. As she looked at her mother, wearing a skin tight v-neck and a skirt two sizes too small, Kennedy said dryly, "You're right. What you're wearing is so classy. But if you were worried about me...tempting that pervert, maybe you should have stayed home instead of running around town and spreading your legs for anybody who'd have you."

Her face turned red and Kennedy braced herself as her mother stormed towards the porch. But Kelly stumbled and ended up on her hands and knees. "Damn it!" Kelly sobbed out, slamming her fists into the porch. "It's not right, damn you! You end up with...with *this*...and I don't have anything!"

With a smile, Kennedy shook her head. "I get it now." Crouching in front of her mother, she said quietly, "I was given this house by two people who loved me, who thought I was worth taking care of, worth protecting. You...you left me alone in the emergency room when I was black and blue from what *he* did to me. You didn't care. If you're jealous of what I have, you only have yourself to blame. I wouldn't have ended up with them if you were any sort of parent. Now get off my property before I call the Sheriff's office."

With that, she stood up and walked away, closing the door quietly behind her. She clicked the deadbolt and lingered there for a moment, pressing her brow to the door as she took a slow, steadying breath.

Finally, a smile spread across her lips. It was over—for fifteen years, leftover feelings for her birth mother had kept her from completely moving past her rape. She'd blamed her mother, yes. She couldn't deny that.

But she didn't need to do that any more—she could put it completely behind her.

Jack...and her mother.

Duncan scowled as he pulled up behind one of his deputies. The car in front of the cruiser was a familiar one. Duncan had pulled it over more than once himself.

Life hadn't been kind to Kelly Masters. In the past fifteen years, she had gone from a fairly attractive, if somewhat trashy, looking woman to a woman with lines no amount of make up could hide. Her hair was brassy and dry and there were huge bags under her eyes. Her teeth were stained yellow from tobacco and she always smelled like a bar.

Stale smoke and alcohol.

As Duncan climbed from the car, he could hear her yelling at the deputy from fifteen away.

Her car was stuck—no way was it getting out of the ditch. But Kelly didn't look too interested in climbing out of it. Duncan could hear the wail of sirens far off and knew they were all going to have their hands full dealing with this bitch.

Damn it, he wanted to be at Kennedy's. Wanted to make love to her one more time before he had to turn on the lights and explain.

Instead, it looked like he was going to have his hands full with her stone bitch of a mother.

"Damn it, it's not my fucking fault...there was a cat in the road..."

CHAPTER ORNAMENT

Kennedy watched as her mother sped down the lane, the car weaving back and forth. Disgusted, she turned away from the window and walked over to the phone. Kelly was going to hurt somebody if she stayed on the road too long.

A few minutes later, she hung up the phone and she stood there, staring around the living room, staring at familiar pictures. Cole and Lisa, on their trip to Hawaii. Lisa standing with Kennedy on the rim of a deep gorge—the trip to the Grand Canyon.

Minutes passed and she finally turned away from the pictures and headed for the kitchen.

She needed more wine.

The skin on the back of her neck prickled and she spun around with a smile on her face.

But the shadow standing in her hall was all wrong. She shivered as a cool wind blew in through the open back door. Swallowing, she stepped back and the shadow advanced, stepping out of the darkness of the hall with a smile on his face.

"Zane. What are you doing here?"

He smiled at her, a slow friendly looking smile. But there was a light in his eyes that made her skin crawl. "You shouldn't have done it, you know," Zane said, his voice friendly and level. "You should have just left...or never come back to begin with."

He paused, casting a look around the house, his mouth twisting into a snarl. "Maybe I should have burned this place to the ground—then you'd have even less to come back to."

Fear curdled in her belly but she forced herself to stay calm. "Zane, I really don't understand."

"Of course, you don't. Not now. Not ever." He stepped towards her, his eyes gleaming. "You see, I'm not going to let him do this. He can't destroy the Pride. And that's what will happen if you become his mate. You'll destroy him. That's what humans do to our kind. And I won't let you destroy him."

*Destroy the pride? What in the hell...*Her voice shook a little as she said, "Destroy who? I don't know what in the hell you're talking about."

Zane shook his head. "I know—it's no surprise. Humans are pathetically weak, stupid. They always have been. My wife was the same way, weak and stupid. I had to get rid of her—I waited until she had Casey. Wanted to see if the baby was mine. She was. Good thing, otherwise I would have killed her too."

"Zane, your wife died in childbirth. Lisa told me that," Kennedy said. She took another step back but she couldn't go any further. The gleaming oak of the butcher block was at her back and Zane was entirely too close now.

He smiled. "No, she didn't. She was bleeding, I know. But I could have gotten her to the hospital. They could have saved her. But I didn't want that whoring bitch around, not when I had a daughter to raise. Casey was one of us and I wasn't going to let her mother's weak blood ruin her."

Kennedy blinked away tears as horror wrapped a fist around her heart. "You let your wife die?"

Zane nodded, his face blank and empty. "I didn't just let her. I stood there and watched. Of course, not the entire time. I had to clean up Casey. But once I knew she'd lost enough blood, I called the ambulance. They got there just as she died and I stood there, holding my baby and crying, pleading with them to save her. I'd just gotten in, you see. Can't you save her...?" He mimicked the voice of a man lost in frenzy of grief and then he smiled.

Shaking her head, Kennedy whispered, "You're crazy."

He just shrugged. "I do what I have to, Kennedy. And what I have to do is protect the Pride. Duncan needs a mate who is one of us. Not a human." Reaching out, he caged her with his arms, leaning into her body.

Icy tongues of fear lashed at her and Kennedy shrank away as he bent down and nuzzled her neck. "Duncan—what in the hell does he have to do with this?"

But even as she asked, she knew.

*Duncan...*it was him. He'd been the man she'd slept with last night. She should have known—those odd golden eyes...And she would have recognized him, if it hadn't been for his voice. He'd lowered it...made it sound deeper, barely spoke above a whisper. Disguising it just enough to keep her from recognizing him.

"You didn't know," Zane mused, chuckling. "I knew you didn't know the whole truth of it, but I thought you at least knew who he was." He pressed his hips against her and she felt the hard length of his penis against her belly. "I didn't figure you for somebody to fuck a man without even knowing who he was." He trailed his hand up her neck, fisting there in her hair as he smiled. "Maybe you're more like your mama than I thought. Of course, you're quite a bit prettier. And you don't stink of other men."

Kennedy tried to jerk away, but his hand tightened in her hair and leaned more heavily into her, effectively keeping her from moving away. "Maybe I'll have a taste of what it is that has Duncan so determined to have you."

"Let me go," she whispered, trying to shove him away. It was like shoving at a brick wall.

"No." He lowered his head and licked at her neck. "Don't worry about Duncan. I'll take care of him—that's what I do. And in a few years, I'll make sure he finds a mate. A woman worthy of him."

Tears burned her eyes. "What—are you going to pick her out for him?" she spat, still struggling to get away.

Zane laughed. "I already have. Casey will make a perfect mate for the leader of the Pride. And we'll keep any more weak, human blood from tainting our people."

With a scream, Kennedy shoved at him with all her might. "Damn it, let go of me!"

His hand tightened in her hair to the point of pain. She saw red and turned her head as much as she could, sinking her teeth into his forearm and biting.

She bit until she tasted blood and then she went flying. As she shoved herself up from the floor, she found him staring at her with a smile. Like a cat, toying with a mouse...

"Oh, I liked that," he murmured, lifting his arm and licking the blood away.

The gesture looked almost feline and she shivered as he lifted his head and stared at her. Holy shit...his eyes were glowing.

"We like it when our mates bite, Kennedy. I think I understand a little of what he wants so bad—I almost regret taking it away."

Duncan held his body absolutely still, even though he wanted to tear inside the house and gut Zane. He couldn't completely control his rage—his hands had Changed, and as he turned and pressed one palm to the door, black claws glinted.

He was scared to move—the one brief glance he'd had into the window had shown him that Zane had cornered Kennedy. With him standing that close, Zane could break her neck in a second.

"Don't worry about Duncan. I'll take care of him—that's what I do. And in a few years, I'll end make sure he finds a mate. A woman worthy of him."

Duncan clenched his eyes closed and prayed for a miracle as Kennedy hissed out, "What—are you going to pick her out for him?"

Zane's laugh made cold chills run down Duncan's spine.

He's completely insane, Duncan realized.

And what his lieutenant said next only made Duncan's blood chill even more. "I already have. Casey will make a perfect mate for the leader of the Pride. And we'll keep any more weak, human blood from tainting our people."

Kennedy screamed and he heard the soft sounds of struggle as she tried to move away from Zane. Then Duncan heard a soft, harsh intake of breath and the scent of male hunger spiked.

There was a crash and Kennedy cried out. The sound was closer. Duncan eased inside and saw her lying on the floor, staring in front of her with horror on her face.

"I liked that. We like it when our mates bite, Kennedy. I think I understand a little of what he wants so bad—I almost regret taking it away," Zane said.

Duncan could see the shadow of the man moving closer to Kennedy and he sprung, placing his body between Kennedy and the man who'd been like a second father to him.

"Oh, you're going to regret a lot of things, Zane. But not for long."

Kennedy screamed as Duncan suddenly appeared in front of her. Then relief overtook her and she felt trembles of shock starting to settle in.

She scurried back, scooting back on her butt and pushing with her heels. "Duncan...oh, God."

He didn't look at her. "Why don't you get out of here for a few minutes, Kennedy? I'll handle this."

Zane snarled—the sound wasn't remotely human. "If you had *handled* it, I wouldn't have to do this."

Duncan shook his head. "You aren't doing this."

Zane grinned at Duncan. "Don't count on it, cub."

Cub...

And then Zane leaped. What happened next was something that didn't make sense to Kennedy's terrified mind. It wasn't a man that landed on Duncan.

It was a cat. One of *those* cats, huge, snarling, and deadly.

Duncan punched at the cat's head and the beast went flying. He stood up and Kennedy swallowed, hardly able to breathe, as something happened to Duncan.

He was...he wasn't...*oh, shit.* She keened and the sound made her jump. Clamping her hand over her mouth, she stared at the huge cat that stood in Duncan's place.

The cougar cast a look at her over one massive, muscled shoulder and she found herself staring at the cat she'd seen just a week before, when she'd woken up on the forest floor. Duncan—

He lunged for the other cat just as it started to move towards Kennedy. Burying her face against her knees, Kennedy tried to block out the snarls, the hisses and growls.

"Come on, sweetie..."

She felt gentle hands on her shoulders and cried out, trying to back away before she even looked up. It was the medic—Kennedy remembered her—when she had woken up in the ambulance a week ago, this woman had been crouched over her, cleaning up the various scrapes and scratches. Her dark liquid eyes stared at Kennedy with sympathy and used her body to keep Kennedy from looking where the two cats continued to battle. "Come on, honey. You don't need to see this. Duncan will be fine."

"Duncan..." She turned her head, but the woman caught her face with a gentle, unyielding hand.

"He can handle this, Kennedy. It's what he does."

It's what we do... The words eerily echoed the ones that had been murmured to Kennedy just a few nights ago. Looking up, she saw nothing but concern in the woman's dark eyes. Slowly, she reached out and let herself be helped to her feet.

As a scream sounded through the air, Kennedy flinched, but the woman continued to guide her out onto the back porch.

She stilled as she realized there were others out there. Samuel Pride, she'd gone to school with him, shared classes with him in high school. Glenna McGuire...and more. Even as she watched, more and more people trickled out of the woods until her backyard was so full of men and women...and *children*...they had to stand shoulder to shoulder.

Even when no more bodies could fit, they drew close, crouching on the low brick wall, even crouching in the tree limbs. Two young men, identical, from their silvery gold hair down to the heavy boots they wore on their feet, stood closest, waiting at the bottom of the porch steps and staring in the door of her house with an expectant look.

There was one more scream. Kennedy licked her lips as silence fell.

There was a soft sound, a clicking on the brick patio porch and she turned her head and found herself staring into golden yellow eyes. The cougar was bleeding from half a dozen small wounds but he didn't seem to pay any attention to them as he padded a little closer.

Kennedy backed away a step, shaking her head.

The cat stilled and sat down on his haunches. She felt something tighten in the air around her—it was happening again. She heard wet, cracking sounds, a harsh gasp of breath—and then the cat was gone.

And Duncan was kneeling on the patio. He lifted his head and stared at her from golden yellow eyes, regarding her somberly.

Kennedy blinked. "Am I going crazy?" she whispered softly.

Duncan shook his head as he stood slowly. "No. You're not crazy." He briefly glanced at all the people gathered in her backyard with a faint smile. "Although I can understand if you'd prefer that."

"You were the man here last night," she whispered.

"And the night before." Thick lashes covered his eyes for a moment and he lowered his head a little. "I was going to tell you tonight."

"Tell me what?" she asked weakly. Gesturing toward her house, she said, "A little late night breaking and entering is nothing compared to this."

He stared at her, the expression on his face uneasy. "I was going to tell you as much as you could handle—tonight. But I would have told you everything."

Kennedy breathed out shakily. "Who are all these people...what are they doing here?"

"That's the Pride." Duncan smiled at the woman who had helped Kennedy out of the house as she moved past him, lowering her head in a deferential nod. "They came because they might be needed."

"Needed for what?" she asked weakly. "Is there a parade or a party I don't know about?" Why would *that* many people be needed? There had to be at least a hundred of them. No...more.

"Needed to protect my mate." He moved a little closer and when she didn't back away, he closed the distance between them.

Warm, strong arms closed around her and she tipped her head back to stare up at him. "Mate?" she repeated a little dumbly.

He nodded, lowering his head to skim his lips across her cheek. "Yes...my mate. You. Unless—unless you don't want me."

She heard the doubt in his voice. Slowly, she wrapped her arms around his neck and whispered, "How I could not want you? I came back here to find you."

As his mouth lowered to hers, she heard the people all around them break into laughter.

Epilogue

So she was more than a little nervous, that was understandable, right?

Staring at her reflection, she told herself she had good reason to be nervous. Hell, it wasn't like she got married every day.

A funeral, her wedding...all in one week. She bit her lip, recalling said funeral in vivid detail. It hadn't been a public one—in fact, it was one the vast majority of people would never even know happened.

There was no way to explain away what had killed Zane Matthews, not without the Pride risking exposure.

He'd been burned. Kennedy had been there—Duncan had refused, but she insisted. Zane had meant a great deal to Duncan and she suspected it had torn a hole in his heart, what had happened. Oh, she knew he didn't regret it, but not regretting it and not hurting over it were two different things.

Kennedy had to admit, she'd been a little surprised as Duncan confessed what would be done with the body. Bones never burned completely away.

"Human bones," he'd told her. "We're not human..."

No. No, they weren't. The three hundred people who had crowded into her back yard weren't human, but they were going to be her family. Married into a pride of mountain lions, she thought with a faint smile.

"You look amazing."

She jumped at the sound of Duncan's gruff voice. He hadn't been disguising it those nights. Strong emotion had an effect on his voice, making it rougher, deeper...she'd learned that over the past few days. Anger, hurt...*hunger*...

And judging by the gleam in his eyes she suspected she knew what had caused it this time.

He reached up, toying with the light switch, a faint grin on his mouth. Narrowing her eyes, she turned around and glared at him. "Don't even think about it," she said haughtily, crossing her arms over her chest.

Duncan continued to toy with it, still smiling. "Why not?"

Kennedy just arched a brow at him.

His hand moved, leaving the light switch to thoughtfully stroke his chin. "Okay, maybe I won't. If you'll take that nightgown off. It's too pretty for me to rip off."

Kennedy felt the blush start low on her chest and spread upward until her entire face was flaming. Uh...*strip*...She glanced down at the silvery blue silk nightgown before looking up at him. "Okay, you can turn off the light."

He laughed softly as he crossed over to stand in front of her, draping his arms over her shoulders. He kissed her lightly and Kennedy felt her entire system burn from that light contact. "No," he murmured as he lifted his head and started to toy with a lock of hair. "I think I want you naked. *With* the lights on."

She gulped. Stripping in front of him—she wasn't sure if she could do that. *Get a grip—he's already seen you naked.*

The other part of her mind argued sulkily, *Doesn't count— the lights were off.* And that even sounded foolish. Duncan could see things clearly in the dark—as clearly as she saw them in the day.

His hand cupped her chin and she slowly lifted her head to stare at him. Duncan stroked his thumb across her lower lip, gazing at her thoughtfully. "Are you okay? I know this past week has been a little...weird for you."

A laugh bubbled out of her throat. "A little weird?" she repeated. "Oh, it's been more than that." Stepping a little closer, she rested her head on his chest. "My entire life has been changed around—all in a week."

He went completely still—for a second, it was almost like even his heartbeat and breathing had stopped. Then he fisted a hand in her curls. "Did we go too fast?"

Looking up, she smiled a little as she reached up and pushed her fingers through his hair, watching as it fell back into place, gleaming like black silk. "It happened fast—but I feel like I've been waiting my whole life, just to stand here. Yes, things seem a little bizarre, but Duncan, I'm not sure I'd understand how to cope with *normal*. I tried for a few years and it just didn't work."

Tension seemed to ease from his body and his arms banded tight around her as he lowered his head, burying his face in the curve of her neck. "I love you—I think I knew it that first day I saw you in the bookstore. I'm not ever letting you go, Kennedy."

He lifted his head as he said the last words, staring into her eyes. Kennedy rose up on her toes and pressed her mouth to his, murmuring against his lips, "I'd like to see you *try* letting me go."

Duncan slanted his mouth across hers and she opened for him, growing drunk on his taste as he pushed his tongue inside her mouth. His hands lifted her and she automatically locked her legs around his waist.

That action left her open and vulnerable. The short, loose skirt of her nightgown rode up as he rocked his hips against her until she was riding the thick ridge of his cock. Just the thin cotton of his low-slung lounge pants separated them. Through it, she felt his cock jerk, throbbing against her.

Cool wood pressed against her back and her eyes flew open. He'd turned and pressed her against the door of the bathroom closet. His hands stroked up her thighs before he reached behind and unlocked her ankles. Kennedy groaned, frustrated as he lowered her to the floor, but then she felt her heart leap in her chest as she watched him reach for the waistband of his pants and shove them down over his hips.

His cock jerked as he straightened and kicked the pants away, arrowing upward, pressing flat to his belly. Kennedy reached out, closing her hand over him, rubbing her thumb across the head. He moved into her touch, a soft growl falling from his lips.

His eyes stared into hers, glowing, burning. She smiled a little as she dragged her hand up and then down. He clamped his hand around hers, leaning into her, using his grip to tighten her hold around his cock as he began to shuttle his hips back and forth.

A shiver raced down her spine as he raked his teeth across her neck before moving up and catching her earlobe, biting down gently. "Mine," he growled into her ear as he continued to pump his hips, moving his cock back and forth.

Kennedy tightened her hand and a ragged breath burst from his lips. He moved, his hand going to her wrist, pulling her away from him. Then he brought her hand upward, placing it on his shoulder. As he lifted her again, she wrapped her other hand around his neck, clinging to him. He pressed against her again, naked this time.

She whimpered as he stroked his length back and forth over her, once, twice, and then he shifted, changing his angle and pushing inside her. Arching against him, Kennedy screamed out.

Her legs locked around his waist, hugging him tightly to her as he started to thrust inside her—slow, deep thrusts—pulling out until he nearly left her, then surging back inside, slow and thorough.

"Kiss me," he muttered and she turned her head blindly, meeting his mouth. She bit his lip and he bucked against her as a shudder wracked his long, powerful body.

The hands gripping her hips tightened, damn near bruising her, when she slid her tongue out, tracing the outline of his lips before pushing inside his mouth, seeking out more of his taste.

He slammed into her, one arm hooking under her knee and opening her further. The rhythm of his thrusts went from slow and teasing to quick, demanding. Each slide of his body against hers had him pressing against her clit. Those maddening little brushes tightened her body and the heat inside her belly threatened to bubble out and burn them out.

Then he touched her lightly, shifting so he could circle his thumb once around the aching bundle of nerves. At the same time, he buried his length completely inside her sheath. Duncan tore his mouth from hers and she sobbed, trying to bring him back to her. But he lowered his head to her neck instead, setting his teeth into the curve where neck joined shoulder and he bit down.

She came. Screaming out his name as fire blistered through her, Kennedy bucked and shivered in his arms. Duncan swelled inside her and the sudden jerk of his cock, followed by the rhythmic pulses as he climaxed, set off another orgasm.

Too breathless to scream, all she could do was moan as it wracked her entire body and left her trembling in his arms. He murmured her name and Kennedy turned her head, pressing her face into his chest.

He shoved off the wall, still holding her, his cock still sheathed inside her body. He stumbled a little and laughed. "Damn it, you make me weak," he mumbled.

They fell onto the bed and she cuddled atop his chest, smiling a little. "I love you," she whispered. Her eyelids felt heavy—the emotional upheaval of the past week was weighing on her and she knew she was going to fall asleep any second.

His arms tightened around her and he muttered one word just before sleep rushed up and claimed them both.

"Mine..."

Malachi

Chapter One

Long after his memories of her face faded, Malachi could still remember the way his mother's voice sounded as she sang him to sleep. Her voice had been magickal. It had soothed away countless nightmares, had sung silly songs that made him laugh, could heal almost any hurt.

Truly heal. Malachi's mother had been magick. He was centuries old before he understood just exactly what she was, a witch—one with Healing powers.

Too bad she had not been able to heal herself.

Malachi had been hiding with the animals when it happened—he had seen it all. Watched as the big men took his older sisters, laughing and fighting off the furious efforts of their mother. Watched as she stopped trying to fight physically and resorted to the power nobody ever spoke of. Fire had struck one of the big men square in the chest.

But there were too many. Malachi could remember screaming as somebody stabbed his mother in the back, the bloodied end of the knife coming through the front of her chest.

They'd found him hiding then. But even if he had not screamed, they would have found him. The men had come to the small village looking for merchandise. Slaves. They'd chosen a good time—when most of the men were not there.

What men remained behind had been slaughtered. Any woman who fought too hard was slaughtered.

He had no idea how old he was when that happened. Time had no meaning for a child that young—and even less for a slave.

Malachi did not remember much, but he did remember her voice.

And as the whip came flying through the air, coming down on his back, he tried to focus on the memory of that voice. The pain from the lash was not immediate. It took a few seconds before it began to hurt, usually right as the whip came cracking down again.

Blood ran in rivulets down his back. He could smell it.

The whipping was worse this time. They got worse every time. The sadistic bastard who owned him would likely kill him.

All Malachi could do was hope it would happen soon.

⁂

But the death he prayed for did not come.

No longer the skinny boy he had been when the Master had first purchased him, Malachi had grown tall, much taller than other slaves, taller than most of the Master's soldiers.

Deeply tanned from so much time spent laboring under the sun and heavy with muscle, he had caught the eye of many of the slave girls. It was a brief pleasure he found when one of them sought him out.

Yet the slaves were not the only ones who had noticed.

The Master's pretty young wife began to notice.

"You better watch it, boy," said Joshua, the slave in charge of the vineyards. It was a sunny day and Malachi had been sent to the vineyards to assist with heavy carrying.

Joshua's face was lined and tanned from years spent under the bright sun, a harsh contrast with the shock of white hair on his head. His tired old eyes held a knowledge that made Malachi leery.

"Why?" he asked quietly, although he suspected he already knew. The Mistress was there. He could feel her eyes on him. She watched him far too often of late.

When Joshua's pale brown eyes flicked the woman watching from afar, Malachi knew he had been right.

"She likes slave boys," Joshua said softly. "No matter what you do when she sends for you, it will not go well for you. Not at all."

"I do not wish to touch that lily white flesh." Indeed, Malachi would rather use his fist than rut on one of *them*. The cruel, selfish people who beat the slaves for the smallest mistake. The Mistress had beaten one of the slave girls just a week ago. Ruth had been heavy with child and the beating had caused her to go into early labor. Both mother and child had died.

All because the Mistress had not been happy with her meal.

Ruth had simply brought her the meal. She had not prepared it. Had not even placed it on the trays she carried to the Mistress.

No. He had no desire to mount that woman.

"It does not matter if you wish to touch her or not," Joshua said flatly. "If you do, sooner or later, the Master will learn of it. And he will beat you to death. If you do not..." The older man's voice trailed off and he reached up, rubbing a hand across the back of his neck. "The last slave who tried to refuse her paid dearly. She told the Master that the boy had tried to rape her. The Master gutted him."

It came to neither.

Just a few days later, Malachi was sold.

The Mistress had not been subtle in her study of Malachi. The Master had noticed. Malachi could remember hearing, "The one is worth too much. I will not throw away the money he could bring me."

It all came down to the fact that Malachi was big and strong, good in the arena.

"He would bring a pretty bit of gold on the block," the slave master had agreed.

So that was where he went.

Sold. Again.

But this time, Malachi actually looked upon it as a relief.

As much as he might wish for death, he did not wish to meet his own by having the slave master cut him open and spill his guts out. A slow, painful way to die.

It was not the first time he had been woken with a foot kicking him in the ribs. It would not be the last. As he rolled to his feet, Malachi imagined grabbing the bastard who had kicked him, knocking his legs out from under him, taking him to the ground and choking the life from him.

The Master was not a cruel owner, especially not compared to the last one who had the fondness for the whip. Still, Mal fantasized about killing him. About running away and living in freedom.

Enough time had passed since the last brutal whipping from his previous owner that the scars on his back had faded from angry red to pale white. None of the beatings he had received since had been as bad—they had not left any scars and none of them had been with one of those damned whips. But Malachi had not forgotten the pain.

And if anybody saw the look in his eyes just yet, he would most surely be beaten. So he kept his head bowed as he waited for the orders.

With this new Master, his life had become routine. Two days ago, he had fought in the arenas. He would not fight again for another five. So he was either needed for heavy lifting—or because it was time to lay with the Mistress again.

He sincerely hoped it was lifting.

The Mistress had a taste for pain that turned Malachi's stomach. Even thinking of what she liked to do during sex made his skin crawl and his testicles shrivel.

He would almost rather step into the arena again. Almost. Since he had been bought by the new Master, he had stepped into the arena many times. He had won each bout.

But winning was not enough.

Taking the life of the fallen fighter had made him ill for days. But the man would have died anyway, and it would not have been anything as merciful as having his neck snapped.

The only good thing about the bouts was the knowledge he would have a respite after each win.

Malachi was wrong. He was not needed for lifting or for mounting the damned Mistress again. By mid-evening, he was face to face with the man in charge of preparing men for the arena. The man was small and dark with slanted eyes and an odd accent. He moved like nothing Mal had ever seen.

"Too slow. Too slow. You too big to ever move fast enough," Yen said, shaking his head as he circled around Malachi. "You no business fighting tonight—still bruised." He poked a slender finger into Malachi's multi-colored rib cage and smiled when Malachi did not even flinch. "Last fight was close miss."

Malachi did not bother saying anything. The man he had fought had moved in a manner oddly similar to Yen's but had stood nearly as tall as Malachi. He had been deadly. A few times, Malachi had seen his life flash before his eyes.

And it had been a pathetic thing, too. Because there was very little in his life worth fighting to live for. All that kept him on his feet had been sheer stubbornness.

"You stiff. Moving slow."

Malachi met Yen's eyes briefly and said, "What do you expect?"

Yen scowled. "No business fighting so soon. Come—have medicine for bruise."

Hours later, Malachi was once more lying on the small pallet that made up Yen's bed. From the knee down, his legs were on the bare earth. The sharp scent of the weird herbs Yen used saturated the air. Thick cloths soaked in the herbs were wrapped around his torso. Malachi knew from experience— Yen's odd concoctions would have his bruises feeling days old and he would be moving around normally in very little time.

But sadly, it was quite likely the rapid recovery would just end with Malachi back in the arena that much sooner.

That much sooner he would have to face down another man and kill him.

He had no idea how many men he had been forced to kill, but their faces haunted him. Many had been hardly more than boys.

There had been a time when Malachi had refused to deliver that final strike. But it had resulted in one outcome—the fallen were still killed, right in front of him, usually in a slow and painful manner. And Malachi was beaten.

He could handle the beatings. He had been raised a slave. Beatings were something he was used to. But the last time, he had watched as one of the centurions eviscerated his fallen opponent. Then castrated him. Those screams would haunt Malachi until the day he died.

How much longer...

Nearly a week passed before he was summoned again. He was left alone, left to heal, left to brood. Malachi was not summoned to the Mistress' bed and he was not forced into the arena either.

When he was finally summoned, he was prepared for one or both duties.

Surprisingly though—it was neither. He was sent to the baths with hardly a word.

Before sunset, he had been sold.

Again.

"Oh, he is worth every single bit of gold you paid."

The new Mistress was not a chore to look at, but the way she stared at him made Malachi feel dirty.

"If he does not please you, we can always use him in the arena," the Master said, barely glancing at Malachi. "That is where I first saw him. I have watched him many times. Julius did not wish to sell him, but I knew you would enjoy him. I paid a heavy sum of gold for him. Julius did not wish to let his best fighter go. He fights as if he were born to do it."

Big blue eyes sparkled as the Mistress ran her hands down Malachi's chest, over his belly, then his naked genitals. Malachi stared steadfastly at the floor the entire time, even when somebody tugged on his hair to try to force him to raise his head. He had been beaten more than once because an owner had not liked the look in his eyes.

Defiance, they called it. Malachi was not completely certain what the word meant, and he cared little. But he tired of the beatings rather quickly and he would avoid them when he could.

The Mistress closed cool, pale fingers over his cock and worked him until he grew erect. She giggled like a child with a new toy and said, "I think there is something else he was born to do. I cannot wait to see just how well he does it."

The Master waved a hand at them, smiling. "Take him, dearest. I have business to attend to."

That business, Malachi learned quickly enough, was his own lover, a blond haired man who was nearly as pretty as the Mistress. The Master was content to let the Mistress do as she pleased with her new toy, provided an heir was produced.

And quickly.

Malachi had been the fifth slave purchased for just the reason. The last four had been put to death for failing the Master and Mistress.

Like a stallion in rut, he was to service her. And he was told she had best get with child.

Fucking her had become something he did without truly thinking about it. Malachi stared a hole into the wall in front of him as he pumped against her, his cock moving a slow, steady rhythm as he waited for her to climax. She liked her pleasures, this Mistress. If he climaxed before she had taken her own release, he would be beaten.

He had been with these owners a long while now, and he had not been beaten once. Making her come was an easy enough chore. Sometimes it was reaching his own climax that was difficult. But it was required.

She had born one child already, and both the Master and the Mistress desired more.

Malachi suspected she was already pregnant again, but that offered no reprieve for him. She had wanted sex almost until she delivered the first babe. No doubt this would be the same.

The Mistress arched under him and her sheath began to convulse around his cock. Her nails bit into his flesh and he could feel the hard press of her nipples against his chest. Now was the more difficult part. Hunkering lower over her body, Malachi blocked out the scent of her, the sight of her, picturing another woman in his mind.

This woman was unknown to him—her face always hidden by shadows, her long, pale body with its subtle curves. But it was *her* he imagined whenever he climaxed. Without thinking of her, he did not know if he could achieve release.

The first time she had come to him was truly the sweetest memory he had. Touching her was a pleasure, not a duty, not a chore and she gave as much pleasure as she received.

At first those dreams had been welcome escapes. But then he began to wish for more than just dreams. Much more.

To truly hold her. To truly touch her.

To know her name.

In his self-induced fantasy, she wrapped slender, strong arms around his neck and cried out his name as she came. *Who are you...*

He did not make a sound as he climaxed and the second it ended, he rolled away and moved to his pallet on the floor. Lying with his back to the Mistress' bed, he closed his eyes.

Perhaps tonight, he would dream of *her* again.

The Mistress was with child.

Malachi stared at the room the Master had led him to. "Yours," he had been told. "We are pleased."

Pleased. Malachi kept his eyes on the floor and hoped nobody could see the sneer.

"Perhaps tonight you could provide some entertainment," the Master said as Malachi finally stepped into the room before him.

Entertaintment—Malachi suppressed a bitter smile. In other words, they wanted to see one of his other skills at the celebration tonight. The celebration was in honor of the Master and the Mistress. The entire household was moving at frantic speeds to get ready for it.

Entertainment—a fight. Truly, he did not understand any of these people. Their idea of entertainment was watching as Malachi beat the life out of somebody.

How was that an amusing thing?

Until then, though, Malachi was allowed to go into his new room and rest. He spent the afternoon lying on the bed and staring out the window at the mountains.

Run.

That was all he wanted.

His mind drifted and he found himself dreaming of *her* again. The room was dim and he could see just the vague outline of her body as she came to him, lowering her warm, soft body against his. She was soft, but there was a strength in her that was unlike any he had ever felt in a woman.

Her laugh rang in his ears like angel song as they mock wrestled, their tussle ending with him flipping her onto her back. She gasped as he touched her. Vicious hunger ripped through him as he covered her mound with his hand and felt how wet she was. Making her sigh and moan with pleasure was a pleasure all its own. Listening to her cry out as he brought her to climax had him wanting to throw back his head and scream out his triumph.

Touching her was like nothing he had ever known. "Who are you?" he asked as he pushed her thighs wide and moved between them.

"Shhh..." She never spoke to him. In all the months since he had first dreamed of her, this was the first time she had any sort of response when he demanded to know more of her.

"Tell me," he urged as he pushed into her. The slick wet tissues of her pussy clenched around his cock like a greedy fist. Pulling nearly completely out, he said it again, "Tell me." Driving back in.

The only answer was a hungry female cry. Malachi tried to pull away—he wanted to have her name before he came inside her again. But he did not have the strength.

Anger flooded him and his control went flying out the window. Hunkering low over her body, he fucked her. He was greedy, quick and demanding—taking his own pleasure without much regard for hers, but she came anyway, arching against him and screaming out his name.

The silky wet folds of her sex clenched around his cock, milking him, drawing his climax out until he thought he would die from the pleasure.

He almost prayed for it. At least if this killed him, he would not have to wake up and know she was not there.

"Tell me who you are," he asked once more, feeling the unfamiliar burn of regret and guilt.

There was silence, but then she finally spoke. Her voice was hollow, more of an echo than true sound. "I am nothing. I am no one. For now—"

"Just your name. Just tell me your name."

"Yours," she murmured, her hands caressing his shoulders. "I am yours."

And then she was gone. Again.

***

"Wake up. Come on, Malachi, please wake up."

Malachi came out of the dream aching. In his gut. In his heart. And between his legs—the thick length of his cock was rock hard and pulsating, although he could feel a dampness on his clothes. Pressing a hand to his flesh, he swore silently. She did this to him always. A witch. That was what she was. A demon. Bewitching him, bespelling him, pleasuring him in his dreams until he spilled his seed like some boy.

He saw the lad standing a few feet away, shifting from one foot to the other, staring at Malachi with nervous eyes.

Malachi could not remember the boy's name. It was Li's youngest. The boy helped his mother in the kitchen.

Li supervised the arena slaves and he reminded Malachi a great deal of old Yen.

Like Yen, Li had golden skin and dark slanted eyes and he fought in the same quick deadly way.

The boy had his father's looks, golden skin, brown eyes, slight of stature and fast—eventually, he would be trained for the arena, Malachi suspected.

Likely Li did as well, which is why the boy still stayed in the kitchens.

"We need more wine."

Malachi scowled. "Wine?"

"For the guests. We have not enough for all of them and the others are all busy."

Fetching wine. Some time later, Malachi was fuming over it as he headed into the village for more wine. The Master had plenty of his own, but apparently none of it was rich enough for the party he planned to throw, so Malachi was once more playing fetch.

Malachi knew his anger was irrational. It was just a walk to town with the cart, easy enough labor. Better than rutting on the Mistress, better than fighting, even better than lifting. But he was ridiculously angered by it for some reason.

He could have refused. It truly was not his job, but if the Master wanted wine and Li's pretty wife, Heta, did not produce it, she would be in trouble. The thought of seeing her take the whip was enough to make Malachi ill.

So he was fetching wine.

Would have been nice if the Master and Mistress had decided on this a bit earlier, though, he thought morosely as he trudged closer and closer to the village. By the time he had made the purchases and loaded them into the small wheeled cart, it would be nearly dark.

And it would be nightfall before he reached the Master's lands.

Run...

Malachi blocked out the seductive whisper. Now might be as good a time as any. He had a little money. Heta had given it to him for the wine and it would be a while before he was missed. The celebration had already begun and Heta could bring out the wines the Master did have—when the guests were drunk enough, they would not care they were drinking a lesser vintage.

It could even be morning before Malachi was missed.

But he kept seeing the fear in the boy's eyes, the gratitude in Heta's.

No. He would not run.

Hours later, he was swearing bitterly as he made his way through the darkened forest. The torch on the cart did a damn poor job of lighting the way. Although he knew these paths as well as he knew the back of his hand, traveling them in the dark, hauling a heavy load of wine was enough to have his anger returning in waves.

Lifting his eyes to the sky, he studied the angle of the moon. His mouth was dry, his belly was an empty knot and he was not looking forward to being forced into another fight.

It was that thought that made him do it.

Abruptly, Mal dropped the handles of the cart and turned, grabbing some of the wine. Jerking the oiled rag from the mouth of the jug, he tossed it onto the cart. Leaving the cart behind, he moved off the path and dropped onto the damp grass.

Tipping the jug back, he let the cool, sweet wine run down his throat. Damn a fight anyway. As late as it was, maybe they had all drunk themselves blind. After a little bit of wine, they'd never know if they were switched from the good stuff to the every day wine anyway, now would they?

For a moment, the image of Heta's face danced behind his lowered lids.

But instead of pushing to his feet and heading on, he took another drink of wine. Then another. And another. He kept drinking until the edge of his mind went blurry and the anger gnawing at his gut finally eased off.

He never noticed when his lids lowered. When the jug fell to the ground with a hollow thunk, he never even stirred.

The woman came to him like a whisper on the wind, moving on silent feet through the trees. The wind blew long golden strands of hair around her narrow shoulders, across her face. She reached up and brushed a strand out of her eyes, staring at the man sleeping under the tree.

She had sad eyes and as she studied him, her expression grew even more despondent. "I am sorry." She moved a little closer, kneeling on the ground beside him. He did not move as she reached out and touched a finger to his cheek. "I have been watching you."

As she sighed, her breasts rose and fell under the gleaming white of her gown. "Part of me hoped that you would never come to me. Each time I called, you turned it aside. Such a strong man."

The deep red of his hair seemed nearly black under the silvery light of the moon. She had watched him, night after night, as he bedded the lady of the house, and her instinctive fear had warred with curiosity. How would that lovely hair feel wrapped around her hands? To feel that powerful body moving over hers? He never once used a cruel hand—she suspected even if he had not been bedding the Mistress, he still would have used such care.

This was not a cruel man.

Did he enjoy making his Mistress cry out in pleasure?

And she had also watched him fight. Yes, she had been watching him for months and months. Fear sometimes forced her to leave, but always, she came back here. To watch him.

He was the one.

In her gut, she knew. Tears thickened her voice as she moved closer, brushing the deep red of his hair back from his neck. "I am so sorry." He started to wake as she leaned closer, and Alys began to sing quietly under her breath, stroking her hands up and down his arms, lulling him back into sleep. It was a lullaby she remembered from childhood, one in a language she barely remembered.

Just the lullaby. It calmed him as easily as it had calmed her and Alys moved in again. But she could not get close enough. Fear snaked through her body but she shifted and drew the long folds of her gown higher, straddling his hips. He felt warm beneath her—

An unfamiliar heat streaked through her and she paused, her hands tightening on his biceps. Her voice faltered and as it did, his eyes opened. He stared up at her with dark eyes as he mumbled, "Did not realize I had drank that much wine."

He reached up, touching the tip of his finger to one fat curl as it lay over her breast. Then he palmed her breast and the heat of his hand shook her to the core. He was gentle, this man was, gentle and persuasive, so unlike what she was used to. She could feel the power in his body and part of her wanted to flee.

But she needed him. Reaching up, she fisted a hand in his hair, baring his neck. Lowering her head, she ran her fangs over the taut golden skin. The rush of blood under the surface called out to her.

But before she could strike, he slid his hands under her skirt and she leaned back, only a heartbeat from tearing away in fear. But his hands stayed gentle as he eased her skirts up. "You smell sweet," he muttered against her skin, nuzzling her breasts through her gown. His hot mouth closed over the tip of her breast and she arched against him with a startled cry.

Pleasure like nothing she had ever felt streaked through her and she fisted one hand in the loose cloth draped across his chest. Fabric tore but she barely noticed because he was busy stripping her clothes away. Seconds later, the heat of his body was pressed against her own cool body.

"I like this dream," he whispered, rising to his knees. Malachi kept his hands at her hips, holding her against him as he moved. He moved easily despite the added weight of her body. "I can see you..."

He took her to the ground and spread her thighs. Alys could not fight down the panic that filled her, but he did not shove brutally inside her. He did not even drop his body onto hers. Instead, he returned to her breasts, biting softly at her nipples, sucking them deep into his mouth. Between her thighs, she felt heat.

When he cupped a big, warm hand over her, Alys moaned. The sound was startling, rough and needy.

But even more startling was how his touch made her feel. It made her feel empty.

She wanted to feel him there.

When he began to caress there, she arched up to him with a cry. Two fingers pushed inside her and there was no pain, just a sweet pleasure that made her hunger for more.

He continued to touch her just like that, pumping his fingers in and out. Alys grew hotter and between her thighs, she grew wetter. That was not completely unknown. She had felt that creamy moisture before, when she had watched him mount his Mistress.

When he finally came into her, Alys exploded, screaming into his mouth.

Malachi was dreaming—he knew he was. Some wine-induced fantasy. Not the woman from his dreams, but certainly someone sweet, someone soft. Someone who wasn't bedding him just to get with child. She was delicate, sweet, almost timid. He had not been with a woman like her before.

Looking into her eyes was nearly as pleasurable as sinking his cock inside her. She stared up at him with an awed, needy gaze. Nobody had ever looked at him with such naked need before.

Since he had no idea when he would have another sweet dream like this, he intended to enjoy it to the fullest. As she climaxed around him again, he slowed his strokes. He wanted her to calm, wanted to watch the fog fade from her pretty green eyes. Then he wanted to watch them darken with need again as he rode her.

Maybe then he would come.

Maybe...

Hours later, they lay under the star strewn sky. Malachi was certain he could not move if he had to. He had stopped thinking of this as a dream some time ago, although if he woke and found himself alone in the woods, it would be little surprise.

There was just something...real about this. Something solid. That feeling only intensified as she rolled atop him again, staring down into his eyes with a sad gaze. "You should rest," she whispered softly. Her voice trembled a little as she spoke.

Malachi wanted to know what made her so sad. But before he could ask, she stroked his cheek. "Sleep, Malachi."

He did not wish to sleep. And he knew he should not. It was time to return to the Master's lands. He would think of some way of keeping Heta from the punishment he had surely brought upon her.

Yes, he needed to return.

But suddenly he could barely keep his eyes open. The bone deep lassitude had turned into true exhaustion and he could not even keep his eyes open, much less force himself to his feet for the long walk ahead.

His lids drooped low and as he drifted into sleep, she started to sing.

When she struck his neck, her fangs pierced his skin easily and he barely flinched.

His eyes were gritty with exhaustion well before sundown. But Malachi would not be sleeping that night. He had returned to the Master's property just as the sun was rising, but all of the guests were already sleeping. Many of them were sprawled on the grounds where they had dropped.

There were empty wine jugs scattered around and the remnants of the meal Heta and the other kitchen slaves had worked so hard on. Already, the slaves were busy cleaning up the mess, but it would take much of the day to clear it all away.

From the looks of it, it had been a very successful celebration.

Heta had tried to ask him what had taken so long, but Malachi merely turned the wine over to her and walked off. Li, however, was not going to be put off.

"Bad night."

"My night was fine," Malachi said, trying to remember it a little better. He remembered grabbing the wine. And waking up. In between? Just little flashes of memory. A soft, pretty voice. Big sad green eyes. A woman with a warm, sweet body.

A dream. It had just been a dream, caused by too much wine. The headache he had now was proof of just how much he had imbibed. He felt groggy, too. Too tired. His head felt too fogged.

"No. I do not ask if you had good night. I tell you, last night was *bad* night. Bad things happened." Li moved a little closer, his slanted eyes narrowing, almost disappearing as he rose on his toes, staring at Mal's neck.

When he reached up and tried to touch Mal's neck, Mal batted his hand aside. "Leave me alone, Li. I am tired."

"You be *still*," Li growled, wrapping his hand around Mal's wrist and squeezing.

Mal felt his bones grinding together and he bit the inside of his cheek as pain streaked through him. "What do you want?"

"What happen last night?"

"I drank a jug of the wine and passed out. When I woke up, it was nearly morning. Fascinating story." Li's hand fell away and Mal suppressed the urge to rub at his bloodless wrist. Instead, he studied the smaller man.

Li was pale and for the first time, Mal saw fear in those dark eyes. "You no go anywhere tonight. No matter *what*," Li said. "You hear?"

Tension tightened between the two as they stared at each other. Malachi took enough orders—taking them from a fellow slave? But the fear he sensed inside the smaller man kept him from saying the angry words that burned on his tongue. "I have been ordered to attend the Mistress tonight."

"Good. That good. You stay *in*side," Li muttered, jabbing a finger into Mal's chest. "Inside."

That was all he would say and then he walked away, muttering and shaking his head.

The pounding in Mal's head kept him from thinking about it for too long. He needed to get his work done fast. If he did not get some rest before nightfall, he would likely fall asleep between the Mistress' thighs.

Chapter Two

He did not get that rest he needed, but fortunately, pregnancy was already wearing on the Mistress. Malachi could see the weariness in her eyes and he knew he would only be needed for a little while.

Damn good thing, too. Malachi was achingly tired.

At first, Malachi thought he was falling asleep. Even as he pumped his hips back and forth, the Mistress' pussy wet and soft around him, he thought he was sleeping.

Dreaming. No other way to explain that soft, lilting voice. He was certain he had dreamed that voice.

"Let me in."

Mal pulled away from the Mistress, staring towards the window. The woman leaned against it, running her hands against the empty air as though something was preventing her from coming in. A hand touched his arm and he looked at the Mistress, half expecting to see fury in her eyes for pulling away before he had helped her finish.

Instead, she was staring at the window as though something held her hypnotized.

"Invite me in—I want to play, too," the woman murmured as she stared at the Mistress.

"Please come. Come to me," the Mistress whispered, reaching out a hand to the woman. There was a look of hunger in her eyes that unsettled Malachi. He knew some of the women he had served preferred the touch of other women, but this Mistress had not ever been like that.

Yet she was staring at the other woman as though she was starved for her. That look was not natural, not for her. Malachi could not dismiss the feeling that the other woman had induced this odd change.

The woman did not approach the Mistress. She climbed inside, the movement oddly graceful, so at odds with what she was doing. Her big eyes stared at the Mistress and she said, "Sleep."

The Mistress fell limply back against the bed, her eyes closed, her chest rising with the soft, steady rhythm of sleep.

When the woman looked at Malachi, her eyes were tear drenched. "I beg your forgiveness. But I have need of you. You...a warrior."

She leaped for him then, moving quicker than anything Mal had ever seen. Her hands jerked Mal against her and he fought, trying to throw her aside. But she was strong. Too strong. This was no mortal woman. Her fangs pierced his skin and it felt— familiar. It did not hurt, but he was infuriated. He could feel the life draining out of him.

Something touched his mind. A soft, soothing touch. *Please...please understand. I am so sorry...but I need you.*

Those words circled around in his head, over and over, chasing him into oblivion. The sadness in her eyes pricked at the anger that filled him. Even as he longed to tear her away from him and stop this invasion, the grief inside her had him wanting to stroke away the pain.

He would kill her.

Malachi felt her calling to him as night fell. He sat just outside the training arena, his back to a huge tree trunk. In his hand, he held a spear. It was sharp, well balanced, one he had made with his own hands.

And he would use it to kill the demon after him.

She called—he could feel it, like she was trying to work her way inside his mind and force him to obey. Like she had done with the Mistress the night before. Malachi waited though. He would not go to her. She could come to him and he would kill her.

When she had appeared at the edge of the trees just after the sun had set, Malachi rose, holding her gaze. Her big green eyes looked so sad.

"If there was another way for me, I would have chosen it," she whispered. She started towards him and Malachi hefted the spear, launching it at her.

It did not hit—she moved like the wind, dodging the spear and disappearing into the trees. There was no sign of her. Growling low in his throat, he followed his instincts. They had always served him well enough—he would just have to hope his luck held.

It did not. Oh, he could catch sight of her. But never move close enough to strike. And what was he going to kill her with? She had taken his spear when she fled into the woods.

With his spear gone, he had nothing but his wits, his bare hands and the small knife he carried at his waist.

He heard her whispering into his mind again and he tried to block her sorrowful voice out. But it came nonetheless. *"If there was another way, I would take it, warrior. Know that."*

"There is another way," he growled. "A path into hell and I will see you on your way."

He thought he heard the whisper of a sigh through the trees and he stilled, lifting his head to stare into the canopy of leaves. Nothing, just the wind whispering through the branches.

"*I am not the first one.*"

Whirling around, Malachi saw the white of her gown as she slipped behind a tree just ahead of him. *There you are, you bitch,* he thought viciously.

But by the time he got there, she was nowhere in sight. Again and again, she appeared *that* close to him, close enough he could almost smell the scent of her sweat.

"*You can kill him, a good man you are. You are a warrior, valiant and strong. I have searched for you for so many years. You can stop him—I know you can.*"

He saw her again, even closer than before. Malachi lunged for her, felt her gown slip right through his fingers. Thrown off balance, he stumbled and hit the ground. His head spun as he shoved himself back to his knees and a bone deep weakness overtook him. The world seemed to spin around him and Malachi swore.

"*You cannot continue like this, warrior. You are weak—you have lost too much blood. Please—let us end this.*" As she spoke this time, he felt that curious nudging at his mind, like he had felt when she had been calling him.

Malachi shoved himself to his feet and snarled, "Not this night. I will not go willingly to a demon." Spying a thick branch, he grabbed it and snapped it over his knee.

"*Please, warrior. I want this done.*"

But he could not see her. Once more, she had disappeared into the forest in utter silence. "Foul bitch," he hissed. From the corner of his eye, he saw a flash of white. Whirling, he launched the makeshift weapon. He heard her soft female cry and guilt warred with triumph but before he could reach her, she turned and dove into the trees.

"You cannot run too far, demon," he panted, a mean grin on his face. She was close. He knew it.

Close—

On top of him. She dropped down out of the tree, her slender body full of that inhuman strength. She took him to the ground, her small delicate hands pinning his arms, her legs straddling his chest. He tried to throw her off, but failed.

This was it, then. After all the battles he had fought, he would fall to a female.

As she sank her teeth into his neck one final time, Malachi roared. It did not take long—his vision quickly grew hazy and what little strength he had left faded. Just before the darkness was complete, he felt her pull away. "Just—finish it," he muttered wearily. Then he felt something at his lips. Something warm, salty.

Malachi tried to turn his head away, but one of her hands fisted in his hair and kept him still. "Drink—you will drink now. I will not lose you. Not when I am so close."

Whatever it was flowed into his mouth and he choked as he tried not to swallow. But some of it slid down his throat. Her hand loosened in his hair and she began to stroke his brow, smoothing his hair back from his face.

"Such a pity that you will hate me. But he is coming—my Master. By the time you have changed, he will be here. And already you are stronger than us both. You will see what he is, why he must be stopped. You will defeat him, and then you can be free. And he will take no other."

Whatever it was in his mouth no longer tasted quite so bitter. A flare of strength returned to him and he opened his eyes. And what he saw horrified him. He was feeding—from her. She held her wrist to his mouth and dark blood flowed from the wound. Repulsion streaked through him and he shoved her wrist away.

But his mouth watered as he stared at the tiny injury, craving more of the blood.

He pushed back from her and rasped, "To my death, I shall hate you." He tried to rise, desperate to run away, but that small bit of strength was gone and he found he could no longer even hold his eyes open.

As he fell into the dark, warm embrace of sleep, the woman murmured, "Oh, I understand, my warrior. So long as you see him dead, I care not."

Chapter Three

The next few days were a hell unlike anything he could imagine. Fever had him sweating for hours, his mouth parched. And then cold—so cold no amount of heat could possibly warm him.

There was pain. Obscene in its intensity, it tore at his bones, feasted on the flesh of his neck and burned at his gums. Malachi would have cheerfully taken the pain of the whip over this, had he any choice.

By the time the cloak of sleep lifted, he was half mad from pain, from hunger and from fury.

And *she* was there. Shoving off the cave floor, Malachi stared at her. Rage was a living, breathing monster in him and as he glared at the demon, the rage became him. He felt something rip through his gums. Blood flooded his mouth. Reaching up, he touched his fingers to his lip and felt a weird bulge there. Opening his mouth, he probed at his teeth. No— they were no longer teeth.

Fangs. He had wicked fangs in his mouth, just like a wild animal.

Just like *her*.

"What have you done to me?" he growled.

She sighed and as he watched, tears rolled down her ivory cheeks. "What I had to. As you must do what you have to."

She stood before him with her head lowered as Malachi moved closer. He waited for her to run, but she never moved.

He wanted to feel her neck snap beneath his hands. Could almost feel it. But she did not run, did not flinch. Did not even move as he reached up and closed one hand around her delicate skin. Under his fingers, he could feel the slow pulse of her heart, the thrum of blood rushing through her veins. He could imagine tightening his grasp, squeezing her neck, feeling bones break.

But she stood there, shivering, terrified—and waiting. Like she knew what he planned to do.

With a snarl, Malachi tore away and dashed out of the cave.

In the depth of the woods, he scented game. It was like a perfume in his nostrils, getting more and more powerful as he drew closer. His mouth watered and there was a throbbing along his gums.

The fangs—they were throbbing, pulsating. And as he drew closer to the animal, that pulsating grew worse.

Just in front of him, he saw the deer, a huge buck with a wide spread of antlers.

Conscious thought seemed to stop. Malachi knew only the hunger and the prey. It took only a matter of heartbeats to take the buck down and it was not until he had sated the burning hunger in his gut that he realized what he had done.

Killed an animal. With his own hands. And drank from it. Even now, the hot salty taste of blood burned in his mouth and he felt almost drunk from the sensation.

Then nauseated.

As the full reality of what he had done struck him, Malachi was overcome with the need to vomit, to empty his guts out onto the ground and try to purge himself.

It will not help.

The soft voice whispered into his mind and he snarled at the invasion. "Can you not leave me in peace even in my own damned head?" he demanded as the woman started to murmur to him.

She was not close. Somehow, he knew that. He thought he could even sense her, faintly. Back in the cave, right where he had left her.

Why do you not kill me and be done with it? she asked.

Malachi shoved away from the dead deer, his legs wobbling a little, his head spinning. Leaning against a tree, he whispered, "Just leave me in peace, demon. Have you not done enough?"

She sighed. He could almost feel it, like a ripple against his skin. *I wish I could make you understand. I did what I had to.*

"Just leave me be."

She left him in peace.

But still, Malachi felt bound to her. Trapped.

Even in his dreams, the sensation haunted him.

When the dream first started, he had welcomed it, but the relief was short lived. Even here, he could not truly escape what had become of his life.

He covered his dream lady's body, as he pierced the soft, wet folds of her sex. Mal took her roughly, urgency, hunger and desperation fueling him. He came inside her, once, twice, bringing her to peak over and over until her screams turned hoarse and her hands slid from his shoulders to rest limply at her sides.

"You're unhappy," she murmured to him as he finally pulled away. He lay on his back, staring up at the darkness as she cuddled to his side.

Malachi snorted. "It is a bit more than that. I have not even the words to explain what has happened."

For a moment, she said nothing. Then her hand started to stroke him across his chest, the touch gentle, as though she wished to soothe him. "I know what's been going on, Mal. There's very little about you that I don't know."

"You know," he said slowly. He sat up, pulling away from her warm, soft curves. Malachi closed his eyes against the dark foggy world that surrounded them.

"Yes. I know. Even before she found you, I knew something would change for you, and soon."

"A warning might have been nice," he muttered.

"Why? So you could laugh it off? Or ignore me? Or worse...try to leave? She needed you. This is your destiny, Mal. It was what was meant to happen."

His destiny—that was a bitter joke. He was destined to spend his life by draining away the lifeblood of others? "Destiny? I was born to become this?" he snarled. He reached up and touched the tip of one fang and it sliced open the flesh of his finger. "To become an animal?"

"You aren't an animal. You are destined to save others. To protect them. You are a warrior—she sees this. I can see it. Every one can, except for you."

"How can you see anything? You do not truly see me," Malachi growled, trying to pull away from the smooth, strong arms that held him. "As I do not truly see you. We are nothing to each other, save for these dreams."

For a moment, she was silent. Then she finally said, "You are everything to me. I cannot control these things, Mal. I am controlled by fate and destiny as surely as you are. Even as your sire is. She did not choose you randomly. She was guided to you."

More talk of destiny and fate—impotent rage coursed through him and he pulled away from her. "How do you know so much of her? Do you watch us from wherever you are? Are you the witch that led her to me?" Malachi demanded.

His body ached at the separation and his cock jerked, throbbing like a bad tooth. The need to cover her once more and sink his length inside of her was overwhelming. Even stronger than that damnable hunger that plagued him.

She was silent and for once, he thought he might get some kind of true answer from her. When she stayed silent, he taunted, "Can you see us? How can you see? *What* do you see? Did you see the first night she bit me? Drunk as I was, I remember little. Can you help me remember?"

She sighed shakily and Mal felt ashamed. He had hurt her.

Whether this woman was real or just a product of his own lonely needs, he did not know. But her pain felt terribly real. Turning, he tried to go back to her, but she pulled away. There was a soft sound in the air, almost like a sob, and then she was gone.

Without her to hold him locked in the dreams any more, he woke. And stalked from the cave without even glancing at the petite blonde woman who was responsible for what he had become.

Nearly two days and nights had passed since he had awoken from that painful fevered sleep. Two nights in which he had hunted down wild game in the forest and fed from them once more. He had not killed another animal, though. Just that first one. The other creatures, a wolf and several rabbits, he had just fed enough to ease the hunger, never sating it.

The hunger was enough to drive a man insane. Or whatever in the hell he had become. He sat brooding, perched on a tree limb, close enough to see the mouth of the small cave. She was in there.

She…Alys. Her name was Alys. He had just learned that a little while ago when he had been trying to block her out again. She had been chastising him for not feeding. *You cannot continue like this,* she had said.

"What in the hell do you know about what I am doing or not, demon?"

I am not a demon—just a woman. I…my name is Alys. There was loneliness in her voice. But he refused to yield to it.

Even if he did feel the echo of such a loneliness deep in his soul.

Another spasm of hunger clawed at his gut. Malachi clenched his teeth against it, slamming his head back against the tree and grinding it against the rough bark.

He almost gave into it.

But even as he started to drop from the tree, he felt something in the air. A tightening, like the air before a storm. But the sky was clear. The change was followed by a rush of anger. It flooded him, drew his skin tight, and the despised fangs dropped down. He wanted to bite something—to tear something apart.

Evil.

The stink of it began to taint the air.

Hearing the soft sound of footsteps, he looked down to see Alys creeping from the cave.

"He is coming," she said stiffly, her lips barely moving. Her eyes were dark and wild with fear, but as she stared at Malachi, she tried to force a smile. "I do not know why you did not kill me—nay, I know why. A valiant warrior I found indeed. Though you have much hatred of me in your heart, you cannot simply kill me. But him, you will…"

Her voice trailed away and Alys clapped her hands over her ears, moaning.

And the evil in the air seemed to draw even closer. It took on a scent. Malachi could smell him. It was a man and the very air around him seemed to be painted with the stink of blood, sweat and fear.

Malachi moved closer to Alys, watching as she wrapped her arms around herself and rocked backed and forth on her heels. "No...he calls me...please no..."

The anger he felt for her seemed to melt away as he saw her standing there, so terrified, so pale. She looked helpless. Even though he knew exactly how strong she was physically, the evil beating at the air around them seemed to batter at her, nearly driving her down.

And then she was on the ground, blood pouring from her mouth and nose and eyes. Her screams sounded wet and garbled as she choked on the blood.

"What is wrong?" he demanded, sliding an arm under her and lifting her body so he could cradle her to his chest.

But she had no answer. She did not even seem to realize he was speaking as she began to struggle against him. "Let me go! I have to go—he calls me."

There was a soft, deadly whisper in the air as she spoke. *Come to me, little toy. Where are you now?*

As the man spoke, Malachi could sense a power there, but like a distant thunderstorm, it did not affect him.

Alys, though, she was terrified. It was though she was compelled to listen to the summons. The frightened woman would have gone running off into the woods had he not been clutching her to him.

"Let me go. I have to go. He is calling me," she pleaded, clawing at his arms. Blood painted garish, dark streaks on her face, trickling down her neck.

Mindless of it, he caught her face in his hands. He fisted his fingers in her hair and forced her to look at him as he quietly said, "Look at me."

For a moment, she stilled and he thought he saw some semblance of sanity in her eyes. "I cannot deny him—he is too close."

"You have denied him. You left him; you came here. Do not let him break you now," he said gently. *Broken—yes, she is broken,* he realized. Anger once more swirled inside him, but it was self-directed. He had been so caught in his own rage he had not seen that she was little more than he.

A slave.

Enslaved by fear to a creature Malachi knew in his gut was far more brutal than any Malachi had ever known. He sensed once more that compulsion that rippled through the air as yet another whisper came from the dark. "Does he force you to come?"

Tears began to leak from her eyes, mingling with the blood on her face. "Yes—he is my sire. He created me. He can destroy me. As long as I hear his voice, I cannot deny him." Her eyes closed and she started to whimper once more, tugging against his hold. "Please—let me go."

Malachi rose, bringing her with him, supporting her body with his. "And if you cannot hear him?"

Alys sobbed. "Then he cannot touch me. But I cannot outrun his command. I had to run for days to escape him before."

"Forgive me," he said quietly. He stroked one hand down her hair and then drew back his hand, clipping her soundly on the jaw. She slumped in his arms, her eyes rolling back in her head.

Lifting her in his arms, he carried her back into the cave and laid her down. He checked her eyes, lifting her lids. She was good and out, likely to stay that way for some time. Along the soft curve of her jaw, there was a darkening bruise. Guilt knotted his gut for a moment, but he could not let her run to this bastard.

Nor could he fight him when he was trying to protect her.

Malachi did not even try to understand the sense of it all. This woman had turned him into something he did not recognize, that he did not understand. He should hate her. He wanted to hate her.

But he could not. He was overcome with the need to protect her when just a day before he had wanted to throttle her.

Shoving to his feet, he strode out of the cave. Empty handed and unsure of what he was facing, Malachi strode into the woods.

The man was waiting. But he looked surprised at Malachi's arrival. He hid it quickly, demanding, "And what have you done with my pet, you mongrel whelp?"

Malachi smiled, his lips peeling back from the wicked, sharp fangs. "She is sleeping."

His eyes narrowed as he studied Malachi across the distance separating them. "You are newly Changed, boy. I feel it. Did she make you thinking that you could protect her?" The man started to laugh, his head falling back as he chortled his amusement. "She did, did she not?"

"Do you intend to laugh? Or fight?"

The laughter faded. "There will be no fight. Get out of my sight now and perhaps I will not destroy you."

The air changed again. Like something was pushing at Malachi. But whatever it was had no affect on Malachi. He felt like he was simply walking through ankle-deep water. Chilled, but nothing else.

Malachi cocked a brow and smiled. "Was that supposed to do something?"

A look crossed the man's face, a look of sheer, utter disbelief. His jaw dropped and for a moment, he just gaped at Malachi.

Malachi lazily scratched at his chest as he murmured, "Well, I guess it was. Am I supposed to cringe in terror? I am no beaten, broken woman."

"Perhaps not woman, but beaten and broken, that you will be soon enough," the man rasped and he lunged for Malachi.

Logically, Malachi realized the man was moving with a speed that was uncanny. But his eyes followed the man with ease and he dodged to the side and came up behind his opponent, locking an arm around the man's thick neck and squeezing. It had little effect—his struggles did not slow from lack of air and that was indeed rather odd.

However, the man could not break away either. It was clear he had no clue about fighting. He could not even manage to break Malachi's grip. Malachi reached for the knife he had seen at the man's waist and he jerked it free.

Then he shoved the man away and braced himself as the man spun around and lunged for Malachi. He hooked a foot in between his opponent's ankles and tripped him. As the man went down, Malachi pounced on him, using his knees to pin the man's arms down.

Pressing the knife to the man's throat, Malachi whispered, "Beaten, am I?"

"You cannot kill me—I am no mortal man," he rasped.

"No?" Malachi asked curiously. He jerked the knife a little, watching as blood welled and began to flow. "You bleed. A man bleeds, he can die."

Eyes half wild with fear and fury, the man spat, "That puny knife cannot kill me. Already it heals."

Much to Malachi's displeasure, he could see the truth of those words. Even though it was full dark, he was able to see that the tiny flesh wound was already knitting together, until all that remained was a bead of blood that still gleamed wet.

"And if I use this knife to hack your head from your shoulders?" Malachi asked casually.

The man's dark eyes flashed. Indeed, they actually glowed and the air grew ripe with the stink of fear.

"So you cannot heal that wound, eh? What else?" he mused, pushing back a little and tossing the knife up and down.

"Wood through his heart."

Alys' voice was quiet and Malachi narrowed his eyes as he looked up to find her standing just a few feet away, one slim hand resting against a tree trunk.

"*Bitch!*" the man howled, struggling with renewed strength.

Malachi reached down and slammed the man's head into the ground with all his strength.

"Wood will kill him," she said softly, and then she swayed.

"You will be silent," the man rasped.

But Alys laughed. "Jacob, I do believe you are too terrified to control me," she said. Her eyes glinted hard and bright and she smiled, a feral looking grin that seemed out of place on her gentle face.

"What else will kill him?" Malachi asked, caressing the wooden hilt of the knife and smiling coldly down at Jacob.

"Fire. Sunlight. Weapons of silver. Or you could hack his head from his body. Perhaps that would be a little messy." She pursed her lips, considering.

Without even glancing at the sky Malachi said, "Sunrise is too far away. And I would guess it is just as deadly to us. I do not fancy having to wash his stinking blood away, so we will leave his head where it is."

"Let me *go!*" Jacob demanded and that pushing came once more, harder, more forceful.

"No." With that simple reply, Malachi reversed the knife in his grip, closing his hand around the blade with little care that it would slice his flesh. Lifting his hand high, he brought the worn, rounded hilt of the knife down. Bone cracked. Under the force of the blow, flesh broke and Malachi buried the knife's hilt inside Jacob's chest.

He waited until he saw the light of life fade from Jacob's eyes before he dared to look away. "Is he dead?"

But Alys could not answer. She was too busy sobbing.

Chapter Four

The dream...

In his sleep, while the sun burned overhead, Malachi groaned. *She* was there. The dream woman. Many seasons had passed since she had last come to him, but this day, she had come.

When he had collapsed down onto the piled furs next to Alys, she had already been sleeping. The sun's rising came hard on her and she could not remain awake as the sun began to brighten the eastern sky. Malachi could stay awake far longer and had been out hunting, stockpiling more furs for the coming winter.

After so many seasons in this land, he knew how harsh and brutal the winters were. Malachi would be prepared. While the cold would not kill him or Alys, it was bloody uncomfortable.

"Why do you come to me now?" he asked as his dream woman approached him from behind. He did not need to turn and see her to know it was her. He recognized the scent of her flesh, warm and sweet, as she moved closer.

She trailed her fingers up his spine, resting a pale, slim hand on his shoulder.

I feel a change.

With a snort, Malachi muttered, "That figures." In all the years since Alys had Changed him, his dream woman had never truly deserted him, but she stayed away for long, long periods at a time. Malachi would almost have believed she was jealous of Alys.

There was little question to him, though. If *she* came to him, he would leave Alys. He would find her a protector and he would leave, spend his life with this woman who had haunted him for years and years.

It was empty knowledge, though—he knew she would never come.

And he could not see him walking away from Alys, this sweet woman who needed him, just so he could be alone when he dreamed of *her.*

Alys was real—she was flesh and blood. She needed him.

His dream lover was just that...a lover only in his dreams. He could not leave Alys for that.

Truly, he rarely needed to even think on it. While he was with Alys, the dream woman rarely came.

He had even learned to associate her appearances as a bad omen. When she appeared, something dark was coming.

But Malachi did not want to dwell on it—it had been far too long and he needed her. Turning, he pulled her against him. Her mouth opened under his and Malachi thrust his tongue into the honeyed depths, gorging on the sweet taste.

She wore strange clothes, with fastenings and closures that confounded him. He had long since given up trying to deal with them and simply tore them away.

Malachi—there is something I need to tell you...

"Later," he whispered as he tore away the weird trousers she wore. The tough blue cloth clung to her legs like a second skin, cupping her boyishly slim hips in a way that drove him mad. Shoving her thighs apart, he sprawled between her legs and lowered his mouth to the heated mound of her sex.

He licked his tongue up her slit, opening the wet folds. Her hands fisted in his hair and he could not stop himself from looking up the slender length of her body, trying to see her face. All he could see was a pale circle that seemed out of focus and the longer he stared at her, the less he could see.

Just once, he thought feverishly as he plunged his tongue inside her pussy. *Just once I would like to see you.*

Her hands fisted in his hair and she sighed. Her voice was low and rough as she murmured, "And I, you."

Startled, Malachi pulled away, staring down at her. The sweet tang of her filled his mouth and his cock throbbed between his thighs, aching and heavy, as hot as molten metal. "You cannot see me," he muttered, shaking his head in disbelief.

She sighed, a rough, shaky sound. "Never. I would give all I have to see your eyes, just once."

With a rough groan, Malachi settled atop her body, using his knees to hold her thighs wide as he pushed inside her. So it was not all one-sided. She was not trying to drive him near insane. He tangled his hands in her hair and kissed her hungrily. With his eyes closed, he could almost capture an image of her, or what he thought she looked like.

"What have either of us done to be cursed like this?" he muttered. Malachi slid a hand down the outside of one sleek thigh, catching her leg behind her knee and drawing it up over his hip.

With his weight pressing her down into the furs, he drove her hard, riding her until she cried out into his mouth. Her sex gloved him so snug and smooth, tightening around him as she climaxed. Those little convulsing caresses had him spilling his seed inside her, his cock jerking.

But he did not slow down, did not pull away. Malachi lowered his head to rake his teeth along her neck. His fangs scraped across the fragile shield of her skin and he licked at the blood that welled there. She shivered under him, cupping a hand over the back of his head and pulling him closer. He struck then, seeking out the pulsing vein in her neck and sinking his fangs deep.

Her blood was wild. Magickal. Sweet. So damned potent, he suspected if he ever truly fed from her, outside of dreams, it might just leave him drunk.

As her climax rolled through her, her body went limp and lax under his. Malachi sank down atop her, resting his head between her breasts as he pondered that last thought. "Perhaps it is just as well that we never meet. If we ever did, I have a feeling I would cease to think around you."

Trailing a finger down her throat, he added, "Or I would be so addicted to you that nothing and nobody else would matter. Ever."

Her arms looped around his shoulders and he could feel her fingers tangling in his hair. "Why do you think we will never meet?"

Malachi resisted the urge to look up at her face. He would see nothing. "We have not met in the years you have been coming to me."

"You have a lot of years left before you," she drawled.

"And how can you know that?"

But before she could answer, something tore Malachi out of his sleep. The sun had already set.

Alys was gone. He frowned absently as he slid a hand down the spot where she always slept.

There was something she had not told him. His dream lady. She had told him there was something they needed to talk about. He sat up on the piled furs and looped his arms around his legs, staring into the darkness before him.

Against his belly, his cock still throbbed, full and aching from the dream.

Why do you think we will never meet?

The sound of her voice whispered through his mind and Malachi glanced down at his rigid flesh. "You may be wise to wish we never do, witch," he muttered. "For if we do, it is possible you will not be able to walk for a week."

Possibly longer. It would take years to satisfy this burning need.

Rising to his feet, Malachi padded towards the small stream that ran through the back of the cave. The stream was part of the reason they had chosen this particular cave when they came to this land. Mountainous, green, it possessed deep valleys and endless stretches of forest. A beautiful land.

But before he reached the water, he heard a sound. A scream.

His fangs dropped and he whirled, heading down the twisted pathway that would lead to the entrance of the cave. Malachi paused only long enough to grab the bracae he had shucked before heading to bed. It had been his experience that helping a frightened woman sometimes only scared her more if he was naked as the day he was born.

Damned warring people.

The tribes that inhabited these lands were a damned nuisance at times. They were arrogant, proud, constantly seeking new lands. They even traveled south to war with the people Malachi had been enslaved by. That should have made him smile, because they did much damage.

However, they also brought back slaves. Whenever they conquered a people, survivors were made into slaves.

And that infuriated him to no end.

It had been a woman screaming earlier, one who had been taken as a slave and she had tried to escape. But even though it had not taken him long to reach them, by the time he had got there, it was too late. The woman had thrown herself in the bitter cold water of the river. The men chasing her had tried to get her out, but the current pulled her away.

Malachi had found her body. It had taken nearly half the night. She had been a pretty thing, but there had been bruises on her flesh that made him see red. Rape and slavery or death.

What a choice to make.

He would be paying those men a visit, come nightfall, but the girl's pale face would still haunt him.

There was still some distance to go when he smelled the smoke. He also felt it—pain. Burning and hot, like flames licking at his flesh.

But the screams he heard were not his own.

It was Alys.

Nothing left to even say good-bye to.

Malachi released the holy man, watching as the old gray-haired bastard fell back on the pile of straw he slept on. It was the local priest—he did not belong to the man who had been called Messiah back where Malachi had been held slave.

This one, like these people, worshipped trees, the mountains, nearly anything and everything found in the world.

This man had burned Alys.

She had been found feeding from one of the men in the tribe. Some sort of trap had been laid just for her after she had been seen by one too many people.

"How could you have kept coming back to the same place, Alys?" Malachi whispered, his voice husky and rough from the grief he held inside.

They had trapped her in one of the homes and burned it to the very ground. Her ashes were mixed with the rubble of the home, and that was all he had left to whisper his good-byes.

And that was not the only thing that had burnt this night. He had seen the smoke drifting from the mountainside. About half way up that mountain had been where he and Alys had lived and he knew the smoke he had seen was coming from their cave.

The old priest was still staring at him, his eyes wide with fear, but he was unable to scream. Malachi had taken care of that. This man would speak to no one of Mal's visit—he would not even remember it come morning. But Alys' death would not be forgotten, not by this man.

"Did you hear her screams?" Malachi asked gruffly. The priest just laid there, his eyes nearly black with terror.

"Answer me. Did you hear her screams?" This time, he released a bit of the control he held over the man's movement and watched as the man nodded.

A sad smile crooked Mal's lips and he replied, "Good. It was an innocent woman you burned. No threat to anyone." Alys, bless her gentle heart, had not ever hurt a soul out of malice, or even hunger. And Malachi knew firsthand how pleasurable her bite was. "Whatever you think she was, you are wrong. She was no threat. Now, I, on the other hand..."

He reached down and closed a hand over the old man's feeble throat and squeezed, letting the priest feel the strength there. At the same time, he flashed his fangs. "I am the one you should have tried to slaughter. But since you did not, I will make you pay."

The scent of urine grew strong on the air and Malachi curled his lip in disgust. He knew what the man was thinking, could even hear the disjointed thoughts. It was not a pleasant thing, but he could not turn it off, the cacophony of thoughts he picked up from others.

"Calm yourself, old man. I will not kill you."

In good conscience, Malachi could not. Simply by feeling the thoughts of this old man, he knew the man had acted out of a need to protect his people. That was something Malachi could almost admire—if it had not cost him Alys, he would have even respected the old bastard for it. It had taken bravery for him to confront the demon that had been preying on his people—or what he thought was a demon.

No. Malachi could not kill him. The empty years of his life sprawled out in front of him and he wanted no more deaths haunting him while he slept.

But he did have to pay.

"You will hear those screams, old man, every time you close your eyes. And when you hear them, know this—she was harmless. It was like killing a lamb for fear the lamb would kill your shepherd," Malachi said as he pushed deep inside the man's mind, seeking out the place where thoughts lay hidden until sleep.

As the man slept, those thoughts would creep out to haunt him. He would know little peace, for what little time was left him.

And it was not much. Malachi could smell the death on him. His time was nearing.

It would come soon and then the old priest could greet whatever fate lay in store for him once he passed out of this world.

If the man Malachi had heard about all those years ago was truly a Messiah, then this priest would find a fitting judgment waiting him.

No God would smile upon the murder of a harmless woman.

❦

Grief had him roaming restlessly through the woods for the rest of the night.

He had failed Alys.

Over the years, Malachi had come to accept he had a responsibility to Alys.

To care for her, to watch over her. As sweet and gentle as Alys had been, she had not always displayed a great amount of intelligence. She should have known better than to keep returning to the same place to feed, time after time.

"I should have watched you better. Should have protected you."

Bitter guilt choked him and he wanted to rage as his memory taunted him with the flashing echoes of pain he had picked up from her. But he did nothing to try and block the memories. Was little enough punishment for his failure.

Dawn was coming as he perched on an outcropping of rocks over the river. He stared into the rushing white-capped waters broodingly, barely aware of the lightening skies.

It wasn't until he felt his skin itching that he grew aware of how light it had become around him. Malachi lifted his face and found himself staring at the warm golden rays of the sun for the first time in decades.

He had nearly forgotten how pure the light of the sun was. How warm it felt.

The longer he stared at it, the more his skin itched. Some instinctive part of him wanted to cringe away from it, wanted to run. Alys had told him what would happen under the light of the sun.

Skin would begin to burn, and then blacken. Fire would erupt as though something from within had exploded. There would be pain as it charred his flesh from his bones.

And Malachi waited for it. Even welcomed it.

Alys had burned for his failures. Seemed only fitting that he burn as well.

But the only thing he felt was that mild itching. As the sun rose ever higher, his skin blushed a fair pink, but it did not redden with burns, did not blacken, and there was no true pain.

Rising, Malachi stood on the rock and glared into the fiery golden glory of the sun. Snarling, he leaped from the rock and began to pace. "Can not even death come to me easily?" he demanded.

But there was no answer. Just the distant sound the animals made in the woods and the rushing of the river.

Despair hung around him, weighing him down, as he finally turned away from the sun's light and walked into the sheltering dark of the forest.

His simple home was gone. The priest had sent men to smoke it out and to watch and wait in case any more monsters lingered. Malachi could have dealt with them. But he wanted no more blood on his hands.

And living in the cave he had shared with Alys did not appeal to him.

But he found he could not sleep in the open. Even though it seemed the sun was little threat to him, he could not rest so exposed. He took his rest in an empty den, his arms wrapped around his chilled body.

It was a cold, miserable way to sleep.

When sleep came, he was prepared for the dreams. Dreams in which he would hear Alys' screams while his imagination painted him a picture to go along with those horrible, pain-filled screams.

But he did not dream of Alys.

His dream lady came to him, and her voice was quiet and husky with tears. *I am sorry,* she told him, keeping her distance. She wrapped her arms around herself and stood facing away from him. *This is my fault.*

Malachi felt a new chill settle inside his bones as he studied her. "You knew."

I knew something awful was going to happen. But I did not know what it was.

If Malachi had thought he felt guilty before, it was nothing compared to what flooded him now. She had come to him yesterday to warn him and he had ignored it, seeking out the pleasures of her body instead. Had he listened, he could have saved Alys. He would have watched her better.

Instead, he had satisfied his physical needs and then lashed out at his lady in anger, chasing her away. Without her to bind him to the dream, Malachi had woken and whatever she could have told him that might have saved Alys was lost.

You are angry—I don't blame you.

Malachi was silent, seething. His hands opened and closed into tight fists and he wanted to hit something. Anything.

You were right. I was jealous. She doesn't just get to sleep with you. She was able to be with you, all the time, she said and her voice broke a little. *But I want you to know that I would have never wished anything like this. I am so sorry.*

Malachi closed his eyes, shaking his head. His voice was gritty as he replied, "You tried to tell me. It is my fault I did not listen."

She inhaled softly and he heard her moving nearer. Spinning around, he held out a hand. "No. Do not come near now. Please—just go."

And then he was alone, and that was when the torment started. Because now, not only did he hear Alys' screams, he also heard his lady sobbing.

Chapter Five

She was there again.

Malachi came out of his sleep to feel the presence of that woman again. Her name was Rachel—and she was the first woman of *his* kind that he had seen since Alys.

How long had it been since he had lost Alys? Malachi did not know but it had been a very long time, long enough that even the memory of how she looked had faded.

Indeed, Malachi had not seen any men like him until recently. Men had come, like this woman, seeking him out. Telling him that he had a destiny, a calling. But he had to travel to the lands in the west. He did not wish to leave his mountains.

Vampyr.

That was what they said he was. Vampyr. And there were others, many others, like him. Some evil—Malachi still remembered the taint that had hung in the air around Jacob and he prayed the evil ones were not what normally emerged after the Change from human to—this.

It was the evil ones that they needed help with. Help from those like Malachi.

These people cannot hope to fight the darkness that waits in the night, not without us. Join us—help us.

That was what the first man who had come had said to Malachi. They had met in the forest, months ago. It had still been cold then and snow had drifted down around them as the man tried to convince Malachi to come with him.

His name had been Matthew. He had been nearly as tall as Malachi, and his skin had a golden hue that no lack of sun would ever change. Very compelling eyes. Malachi was even tempted.

Just not tempted enough. He had refused Matthew, and every other one that had come since.

But the woman was harder.

There was something very compelling about Rachel. It was not the strength he sensed in her. Although there was a great deal of that. Looking at her, he knew he was facing his equal. He had felt that when he stared down Matthew the first time.

The ones who had come between Matthew and Rachel had been lesser somehow. Malachi did not understand how he knew that, but he knew he was right. Most of them were not as strong as he was.

Just Matthew, and this gentle-looking, pretty woman.

Malachi saw an empathy in her soft brown eyes. A wisdom that did not seem to fit the smooth, young-looking lines of her face.

Standing at the mouth of the cave, he stared down into the valley. Arms crossed over his chest, the wind whipping his hair into his eyes, Malachi could feel the woman drawing nearer and nearer. "Go away," he muttered, but there was no one there to hear him.

And she would not leave, so even if she had been close enough to hear him, Malachi was wasting his breath.

Turning away from the cave's entrance, he stalked over to his bed, straw piled under a thick mat of fur. He flung his length down along it and stared broodingly at the ceiling far overhead.

She had come in his dreams again, his dream lady. After Alys had died, the woman came to his dreams a little more often, but still, Malachi was always prepared for grim news when he saw her. Grim news and pleasure—sad, that. He began to associate sexual pleasure with bad tidings.

Very sad. This was what his life had become.

It is time for you to leave here, Malachi, she had whispered as they lay wrapped in each others' arms. *You have a destiny waiting for you, and it is not here.*

I do not wish to go anywhere, unless you are waiting for me.

She had laughed. The low, husky chuckle felt like a caress along his skin and it made his blood heat. *You can't leave me behind easily. If you go, then I will follow.*

But you will not truly be there, will you, woman? Even before he asked, he knew the answer.

He would not find her there. No matter how much he wished it.

It is not time for us yet. That had been her only reply and it was cryptic, like much of what she told him.

She had been clear about one thing this time though. She felt he needed to go with Rachel.

But this had been home for so long. Leaving it to go elsewhere, someplace away from everything familiar, someplace far away. Malachi was reluctant to even consider it.

He did not wish to leave here.

Those warring tribes he had known as the *Pictii* had given rise to a new people, one that spanned across this wild land. Though still quite anxious for conquest, they had settled down a bit and he had watched generation after generation come into the world, and leave it.

He had watched their sons and daughters grow into a fierce, proud people he admired. They had a rich love for life, for family. They sang and laughed and *lived*.

Watching them actually brought him a bit of pleasure.

They even spoke of him. In low hushed tones over their fires at night, they told stories of the pale giant who roamed the mountains and dealt with the crueler men, those who would rape and kill.

Some said he was the devil, others said he was a creature of God sent to protect them.

Things had changed so much since he had first come here.

The people had not changed so much physically, although he could see some changes in the descendants. Once, many of these people had been blond and fair, but more and more he saw dark hair, darker skin, remnants from the slaves who had been brought back as spoils of war.

Clothing had changed a bit, but not terribly much. Warmer stuff, it seemed and a bit better made.

Many of the changes were not something that could truly be seen, though. The people did not fight as much among each other. A stronger sense of unity. And fewer followed the old ways of worshipping as the old priest who had killed Alys. Most followed the teachings of the Messiah and there were even priests who helped spread those teachings.

Malachi liked those teachings.

He liked the idea that there was indeed something after this life and that as dark as things were now, some place where pain did not happen sounded rather wondrous to him.

It went a bit deeper than that, though. It called to the part of him that remembered being enslaved, that remembered being forced to either take a life, or to be beaten.

And he suspected that the choice he had made was because of those teachings.

He would leave these lands and follow Rachel.

He was needed—he did not so much care for that, but the knowledge that there were people out there that needed help ate at him. So he would go to this *Brendain* Rachel spoke of and see what exactly they said he was needed for.

Perhaps *she* would be there.

His dream woman had told him his destiny waited. In his heart, he hoped and prayed she was his destiny.

Perhaps he would go and there she would be.

Not that he was much expecting that. It would be too easy and Malachi had learned over the years that easy was simply not something his life was meant to be.

After all, if he was not impressed, he could always come back.

This was home.

Yes—he would go. And maybe, just maybe, fate, or God, would be kind to him for once, and *she* would be waiting.

Shiloh Walker

Shiloh Walker has been writing since she was a kid... she fell in love with vampires with the book Bunnicula and has worked her way up to the more...ah... serious vampire stories. She loves reading and writing anything paranormal, anything fantasy, but most all anything romantic. Once upon a time, she worked as a nurse, but now she writes full time and lives with her family in the Midwest.

Learn more about Shiloh and her books at www.shilohwalker.com.

Kindred: The Shadows of Night
© 2006 Ellen Fisher

She eats men like him for breakfast... literally. Book one of the Kindred series.

In a world of shapeshifters, Hart and Katara are hereditary adversaries. But they have to put their enmity aside in the face of a brutal attack from another enemy.

Uniting their peoples is a difficult task, but the real challenge will be working together without killing each other... or falling in love.

Available NOW from www.samhainpublishing.com!

Six Feet Under
© *2006 Mackenzie McKade*

He found her six feet under...and unearthed a passion beyond their wildest dreams

Buried six feet deep is not what Private Investigator Charlene Madison, had expected when she agreed to meet an informant at New Orleans' most famous cemetery. Neither was encountering the devil himself when Devin Leduc rescues her, only to imprison her in his arms. She can't explain her attraction to him, especially once he reveals his secret.

After centuries of darkness, Devin has found his light. Charlene makes his body burn with desire, along with his temper when her penchant for justice and her stubborn nature lead her straight into danger. Together they will unmask a killer and discover a love so fulfilling, nothing, not even death, will quench the flames of passion.

Warning: This title contains hot, steamy explicit sex, ménage a troi, and violence told in contemporary, graphic language

Available NOW from www.samhainpublishing.com!

Samhain Publishing, Ltd.

It's all about the story…

Action/Adventure
Fantasy
Historical
Horror
Mainstream
Mystery/Suspense
Non-Fiction
Paranormal
Red Hots!
Romance
Science Fiction
Western
Young Adult

http://www.samhainpublishing.com